"Well, what did yours look like?"

Kelly produced her valentine, handing it to Bruce matter-of-factly.

He pulled his version from his jacket pocket and handed it to her, scanning the frilly card she gave him. Even though they were essentially trading evidence of wrongdoing, it still felt peculiar to be standing with this woman exchanging valentines.

"I'm so sorry this happened." It seemed like the right thing to say.

"It's not your fault." Her tone was as flustered as his. "It's…well, it's nothing you did. The girls just…dreamed it up, that's all."

Bruce rubbed the back of his neck and looked at the collection of glittery hearts in his hand. "Carly's never done anything like this before. I don't know where they got the idea, frankly." That sounded stupid the minute he said it. He knew exactly where Carly had gotten the idea—that was the worst part of it.

Under different circumstances, Kelly Nelson could be someone he might consider dating. She was, in fact, the first woman who even remotely struck him as someone he might want in his life. If he was ready to date.

Which he absolutely wasn't.

Allie Pleiter, an award-winning author and RITA® Award finalist, writes both fiction and nonfiction. Her passion for knitting shows up in many of her books and all over her life. Entirely too fond of French macarons and lemon meringue pie, Allie spends her days writing books and avoiding housework. Allie grew up in Connecticut, holds a BS in speech from Northwestern University and lives near Chicago, Illinois.

Books by Allie Pleiter

Love Inspired

Matrimony Valley

His Surprise Son
Snowbound with the Best Man

Blue Thorn Ranch

The Texas Rancher's Return
Coming Home to Texas
The Texan's Second Chance
The Bull Rider's Homecoming
The Texas Rancher's New Family

Lone Star Cowboy League: Boys Ranch

The Rancher's Texas Twins

Lone Star Cowboy League

A Ranger for the Holidays

Visit the Author Profile page at Harlequin.com for more titles.

Snowbound
with the Best Man

Allie Pleiter

HARLEQUIN® LOVE INSPIRED®

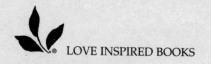

LOVE INSPIRED BOOKS

Recycling programs
for this product may
not exist in your area.

ISBN-13: 978-1-335-42832-5

Snowbound with the Best Man

Copyright © 2018 by Alyse Stanko Pleiter

www.Harlequin.com

Printed in U.S.A.

The heavens declare the glory of God;
and the firmament sheweth his handywork.
—*Psalms* 19:1

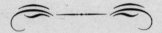

For Captain Kyle

Chapter One

Kelly Nelson thrust a rose into the air and waved it around like a victory flag. "Yes!" She grinned at her daughter, cutting hearts out of leftover ivy leaves on the table beside her. "We got her!"

"Got who, Mom?" Lulu said.

"That lady from the wedding magazine. Samantha Douglas. The one Mommy's been trying to convince since Christmas. She's covering a Valentine's Day event in Asheville, and I got her to agree to come up here afterward. I think she should do a piece on the wedding we're having next weekend."

Lulu grinned. "Yeah!" She sounded so excited that Kelly wondered if she had shared a bit too much of her frustration over getting the attention of the regional bridal magazine. Lulu should never think about how hard it was to keep a business afloat. Eight-year-olds shouldn't give a thought to how old the van was getting or how last month's storm sprung two new roof leaks. Children ought to spend their days happy and secure, right? Lulu could certainly share in celebrating their flower shop's successes, but Kelly felt an obligation to ensure her daughter had no sense of struggle or worry.

"She'll love us. She'll love everything," Lulu added, making Kelly smile.

"Yes, she will. And our valley has lots to love, doesn't it?" In the past year, the entire community of the newly christened Matrimony Valley had put its efforts behind reinventing itself. What once had been a small, struggling mill town had bootstrapped itself, bride by bride, into becoming a quaint Smoky Mountain wedding destination.

And it was catching on. Maybe not quite fast enough to comfortably weather the seasonal nature of the wedding industry, but as one of the leaders of the Matrimony Valley "makeover," Kelly was determined this would be the valley's only lean winter. The coming summer was shaping up to be a promising second "high wedding season"—Kelly had floral contracts for no less than eight weddings between April and July.

Winter, however, hadn't been so busy. Sure, there were life's ordinary floral occasions—birthdays, funerals, anniversaries, parties—but times were still tough. Valentine's Day surely helped, but what would help most was the upcoming Valentine's Day weekend wedding. Without that, it would have been a longer, colder, more worrisome winter. After all, while brides might prefer May and June, heating and water and dentist and mortgage bills showed up all year long. Things were feeling tight, and a piece praising all their town had to offer, published by *Southeastern Nuptials Magazine*, would go a long way toward bringing in steadier business.

"Lots of ladies get proposed to on Valentine's Day, you know," Kelly explained to her daughter.

"That's on Wednesday," Lulu said, pointing to the big red heart Kelly had drawn on the shop calendar.

"That's right. Which means on Thursday, lots of women will be thinking about where to get married."

"And they should get married here," Lulu said with complete authority. Lulu's enthusiastic promotion of her Love in Bloom flower shop always lit a mile-wide glow in Kelly's heart. If she ever doubted she was going to

make it—something she did way too much—
all she had to do was look in her daughter's
eyes. Lulu had hope enough for the both of
them. She always had, Kelly thought with
gratitude. *Even in those dark days. She's such
a blessing to me, Lord. Thank You.*

Lulu's company made Saturdays Kelly's favorite day in the shop. Having her daughter
beside her just made everything bright and
sunny, even if today's skies were gray.

Lulu was lining up the ivy hearts in little
pairs, parading them down the counter in sets
of botanical "couples," while Kelly finished
up estimates and made preparations for upcoming deliveries. A busy week was just what
Love in Bloom needed.

What it didn't need, however, was the ominous buzzing sound and flickering lights that
came from the refrigerated cooler behind her.
*You can't die on me right before Valentine's
Day*, Kelly silently warned the essential ap-
pliance. *You've got to hang on until April, you
hear?*

"Mom, George winked at you again," Lulu
said.

"Why shouldn't George like Valentine's
Day, too?" Kelly had adopted Lulu's theory
that the failing cooler Lulu had somehow
named George was "winking" whenever the

lights flickered rather than gathering speed toward a certain death. *Denial can be its own form of optimism*, she told herself.

Lulu continued her ivy leaf processionals. "Valentine's Day is one of my favorite holidays. Daddy asked you to marry him on Valentine's Day, didn't he?"

These questions were always such a combination of sharp and sweet. If there was one thing Kelly was most proud of, it was how she'd kept Mark's memory alive for Lulu. Her little girl never hesitated to bring her late father into any conversation. It kept Mark with them. And while the sting in her heart at the mention of him no longer stole her breath or made her duck into another room to hide a surge of tears, questions like this still made her heart ache for the love of her life now gone. "He did. And to anyone else, it might have been an ordinary holiday." She gave Lulu a gentle poke on the nose. "But, of course, we never had an ordinary day after that."

Mark had been one of those rare men who could make any day extraordinary. The man could make pancakes a celebration, or a walk through the park an adventure. He'd loved his young daughter—and his wife—with a devotion and an enthusiasm few men possessed.

Mark would have loved the idea of George

the winking cooler. He'd always encouraged Kelly when her flowers were just a pilot's wife's little side business. It gave Kelly comfort to think of him up in heaven, smiling down in the knowledge that his life insurance payout had funded the launch of Love in Bloom as a full-fledged career.

A career she would have loved more with Mark beside her. He'd given her a lifetime of memories, with just too much lifetime left without him to have to survive on memories alone.

"Gone far too soon," everyone who knew him said. They were so very right.

"So now, with Samantha Douglas coming to watch, we'd better make this next wedding extraordinary, hadn't we?"

"It's the reindeer one, right?"

Kelly laughed. "Elk, honey. But that's the one. We're going to host the best elk wedding ever. Maybe the first elk wedding ever, huh?" This particular wedding was not only a welcome end to the January lull, but a creative challenge. The groom was one of the rangers from the local park known for its herd of elk. So much of the decor and wedding elements focused on the elk that everyone in Matrimony Valley had come to refer to the upcoming event as "the elk wedding."

"It's going to be special," Lulu said as she pointed to the corkboard on the shop's back wall. Photos and drawings from Kelly's conversation with the bride showed a bright collection of reds, flannels, burlap and pine. "I like all the red."

"Me, too," Kelly replied. In fact, she'd been delighted at the event's unique backwoods flair. The bride and each of the bridesmaids would be wearing red plaid flannel boleros over their dresses, as well as hunting boots with red lace shoelaces underneath their skirts. The bouquets and centerpieces boasted lots of pine. The whole event was going to be beautiful, inventive, casual and fun.

"It's the perfect wedding for us to show off, that's for sure." Maybe it would even land them a picture on the cover. A *Southeastern Nuptials Magazine* cover story could highlight the valley's commitment to making each wedding special to the couple—to a degree most larger venues couldn't match. "All those phone calls and emails to Samantha Douglas finally paid off." Now the shop—and the whole valley—could take some serious leaps forward. No more George the winking cooler and no more worrying if the roof and furnace would withstand the next cold snap. Kelly was bone tired of adding up bills, squeaking by on materials and saying too many prayers for God to plant them on more solid financial ground.

Lulu slid off the stool as George winked again. "Can I put the heart in the window?"

Celebrate what you have instead of fretting about what you don't. "Absolutely, kiddo." Kelly reached into the drawer below the cash register to pull out a big red knitted heart. Earlier this year, Matrimony Valley's mayor and chief wedding planner—not to mention Kelly's best friend—Jean Matrim Tyler had instituted a little ritual Lulu loved. Jean had knitted a big red heart for each business on Main Street, a large ornament of sorts that could be hung in a shop window.

Whenever any of the businesses in Matrimony Valley—from the Hailey's Inn Love inn to the Bridal Bliss bakery to Marvin's Sweet Hearts Ice Cream Shop or even Williams Catch Your Match fishing outfitters—had good news of any sort, they hung the heart in their window. Sure, it was a tad silly, but Jean was right. In the valley's long, slow struggle to reinvent itself as a wedding destination after the mill closed, celebrating every victory—and sharing those victories with your friends and neighbors—was important. And scoring coverage for this special wedding was a victory indeed.

"Hang it on the special hook so everyone can see." Kelly handed the heart to her daughter. *She reminds me to be thankful*, Kelly thought, as Lulu climbed into the front window and hung the heart right in front. "See any others?"

For Lulu and many of the valley's children, hunting for the hearts was a regular pastime. Just the kind of charm *Southeastern Nuptials* would love to cover. Maybe she should ask Jean to knit up a souvenir heart for the magazine writer to take home.

"Ooh—there's one in Mr. Marvin's window!" cried Lulu. "Maybe he invented a new flavor like reindeer rainbow sherbet."

It would be just like Marvin Jennings to whip up a reindeer-or elk-themed flavor. Of all the shops in Matrimony Valley, his Sweet Hearts Ice Cream Shop had been one of the most enthusiastic adopters of Mayor Jean's Matrimony Valley idea. Patronizing Sweet Hearts was a Saturday tradition for her and Lulu.

"We should go investigate," Kelly said. "Right after I send this estimate to a potential August bride."

"Tell her we're wonderful."

"I will," Kelly promised as she hit the Send button on the email.

"When does the reindeer—*elk* wedding bride get here?" Lulu loved meeting the brides. What little girl doesn't love all the fuss and ruffles of a wedding—even if those ruffles are red plaid flannel?

"Miss Tina, the bride, and Mr. Darren, the groom, both come in on Thursday, the day after Valentine's Day. That's the same day Ms. Douglas is scheduled to arrive, too. We've got a big week ahead of us. But guess what?"

"What?"

"The best man is coming in early—today, in fact—to spend the week vacationing here in the valley. And Miss Hailey at the inn told me he is the father of the flower girl. So you'll have a new flower girl to get to know for a whole week this time."

"That's worth two hearts. Too bad we only have one," Lulu exclaimed.

"I'll talk to Mayor Jean and see what I can do," Kelly replied, delighted to see her daughter's enthusiasm. Meeting any flower girls who came for weddings was Lulu's greatest joy, for while Lulu had friends in the valley, she hadn't really connected with any of the girls in that "best friend" way every mother wants for her child. Lulu's unofficial "flower girl ambassador" role helped to fill that void, and Kelly hoped this wedding's flower girl would be no exception. She didn't want Lulu to feel left behind in all the wedding and Valentine tasks falling to her in the next ten days. Of all the events for Jean, the valley's usual chief wedding planner, to be out of commission for, this one posed the biggest challenge. Jean was right, however—no hired-in planner could handle an opportunity so tailor-made for Matrimony Valley. Kelly would have to step up and serve as both florist and chief planner for this wedding. A whole week with a fun new friend could be the answer to this busy single mother's prayer.

Lulu looked out the window at the inn across the street, where nearly all the town's wedding guests stayed. "I wonder if she likes ice cream."

"I think every little girl likes ice cream." Kelly closed her laptop. "We do, so let's go get some." She pulled the "back in 30 min" sign from its peg on the wall and hung it on the shop door. Some day she'd have a brand-new van and more employees who could keep the store open for her while she was out. Some day she could take her daughter for ice cream on a Saturday without a hint of worry if she'd missed any business.

With Samantha Douglas covering the elk

wedding for the whole region to see, perhaps that day would come soon.

Bruce Lohan watched his five-year-old daughter bounce on the hotel bed. She'd been totally unimpressed with the pile of newly purchased sticker and coloring books he'd just produced from a corner of his suitcase. He'd spent a fortune on activity books and had a stack of tourist attraction brochures as long as his arm, but Carly's attention was captured by the mountain of flowery fabric on her bed. Flowers and ruffles. Her little-girl fascinations were growing more foreign to him all the time.

"This bed has so many ruffles, Daddy," she said as she bounced. "Can I have one like it at home?"

"I'd never find you in all those ruffles. What would anyone do with a pilot who…lost…his own daughter?" His voice hitched just a bit on the word *lost*, the way it always did when the ordinary word popped up in conversation. *Lost* stopped being an ordinary word when Bruce "lost" his wife to cancer two years ago. The thought of losing Carly—even as a joke among a mountain of fluffy fabric ripples—was enough to make his heart momentarily ice over.

He pulled up his mental checklist of father-daughter vacation activities. "Shall we go for a walk and see how the waterfall freezes over?"

"Nope," she declined, flopping down from the incessant bouncing to run her fingers along a pillow's line of tassel trim. "I'm fine."

"Well, then, let's go exploring for animal tracks in the woods. You can wear your new boots."

Carly rolled over onto her back. "It's cold outside." She wiggled her fingers up in the air. "My fingers'll get all numbly."

Numbly. Back in Sandy's last days, Bruce remembered praying for numb. Pleading for God to make the pain to stop so that each breath wouldn't feel like swallowing fire. Now, he wasn't sure his ever-present "numbly" was any gift at all. These days, the only things he could honestly say he felt were instantaneous pangs of fear and loss. Pangs that kept poking up in his life like trip wires, driving a need to stay busy that bordered on compulsion.

Action was the only defense he had. Motion was his best protection against the niggling sensation that one of these days he'd stop feeling altogether. Except for Carly. Sweet, precious Carly. There were stretches where the fierce love he bore her felt like the only fixed thing keeping him upright. The only feeling he still possessed. And yet, even that came with the suffocating ache that his grief kept him from loving Carly well. Or right. Or enough. Losing Sandy had hollowed him out inside. Raising Carly seemed to require so much more from him than he had to give.

"Dad," Carly moaned, her blond head surfacing from behind a tidal wave of ruffled pillows.

"What?"

"You went away again."

How poor was a father's lack of focus if even a five-year-old could pick up on it? No matter how he tried to hide it behind a busy day of activities, Carly still knew when his thoughts of Sandy's absence pulled him under.

It was so much easier to hide at work. The precise demands of helicopter piloting were almost a release from the fog of daily interaction. In the air for the Forest Service, Bruce could be engrossed, analytical, responsive, almost mechanical. On the ground, where he had to be human, everything stymied him. He couldn't hope to be happy, so he settled for busy.

But busy wasn't happy. He had to start finding his way toward happy, or at least away from numb. This trip was supposed to help do that, but they'd been here one hour and already he felt as if he was just spinning wheels.

"Well," he said to Carly, hoping he masked his sense of emptiness, "we can't just sit around. You were sitting in the car all the way here." He'd tried to make the drive an event in itself, taking Carly up North Carolina's scenic Blue Ridge Parkway on the way to Matrimony Valley. The plan was that the route would launch the whole trip in a special way. Be more fun than slogging down the highway from their home in Kinston, right?

Wrong. He'd messed that up, as well. It had been a stupid, misguided idea to give Carly hints that there might be unicorns in the vast forest.

Carly's unicorns. If there was anything that stymied him more than his fog, it was his daughter's imaginary unicorns. She seemed to deal with Sandy's loss by imagining unicorn sightings. *Mom sends them*, she'd explained to Bruce when he had asked, breaking the last pieces of his heart into bits.

Sandy had sent him no such signs of comfort. Or symbols that he was doing okay. In fact, an accurate description of his life would be that it was one big, messy glob of *anything but okay*. Maybe he'd gain some sign of approval when he did something to actually deserve it. The trouble was coming up with what that might be.

So, he'd chosen to give Carly more unicorns. He took them on the scenic mountain highway and stopped dozens of times along the way to take in the sights and allow lots of unicorns to make their appearance.

It hadn't worked. At. All.

Instead, Carly grew increasingly disappointed that no unicorns had appeared. How had that happened? How could a little girl's own imagination disappoint her? What did the sightings—or lack of them—mean? He had no idea, but it could hardly be a good thing that Carly had somehow chosen for her imaginary unicorns to stay in hiding today.

He'd failed her, and he couldn't even say how. *Way to be Dad of the Year—I've already botched the first hours of vacation. Not hard to see why Sandy never let you plan outings, is it?*

And there it was, one more item for the long list of things Sandy did better than he could ever hope to. Sandy could plan one activity and make it a golden, memorable moment. Bruce could plan six and not get a single one to "stick." How fair was it that Carly—who had already lost so much—now paid the price for his mountain of deficiencies?

"Hey," she said, as something caught her eye. She rolled off the bed and bounded beyond him to the window, pressing her nose against the lowest pane and peering down at the row of shops along "Aisle Avenue," the town's main street. "Look," she said as he walked up behind her. Carly pointed to a sign hanging from a shop across from them with a picture of a huge ice-cream cone painted on it.

"What does that sign say?" she asked coyly.

It says, "Dad, can we have ice cream?" That's what it says. "It says Marvin's Sweet Hearts Ice Cream Shop."

She turned to him. "Ice cream?" Her words were as sweet as any dessert this guy Marvin could hope to serve up. "We could have some, couldn't we?"

Bruce teased her by faking a yawn. "I don't know. Seems like you'd rather nap in all those pillows. I know I could use a few winks."

"Napping's for babies," Carly declared quickly. "You said we were gonna do lots of fun things on this vacation. So…eating ice cream is fun, right?" She returned to the window and let out a squeal. "Look! There's a little girl like me going inside."

As far as Bruce knew, Carly was the only girl her age invited to the wedding. Her role as flower girl was part of what would hopefully

make this trip so special. Of course, Matrimony Valley was an actual town, not a resort,
so it stood to reason that children and families
lived here. They'd driven past a school on their
way into town. And Carly was right in one re-
spect: eating ice cream was a fun thing to do.
None of his earlier suggestions lit up her face
like it was now, that was certain.

"I don't see why we can't." He took Carly's
hand. "Maybe all the little girls in Matrimony
Valley like ice cream."

"*Everyone everywhere* likes ice cream."
Carly laughed. The sound eased the tight-
ness of Bruce's chest. As they made their way
down the staircase to the inn's lobby, Carly
chatted on about how any girl who liked ice
cream must be nice. Kids made friends like
that all the time, didn't they? Sandy's gift for
friendship was so evident in Carly—every
stranger was someone wonderful Carly just
hadn't met yet.

Go eat ice cream. Go be friendly, he told
himself as they crossed Aisle Avenue. *Shove
yourself back into life this week, for Carly's
sake if for nothing else.*

Chapter Two

No sooner had Kelly settled on a flavor than the door of Marvin's pushed open and a little girl skipped in. Behind her came a tall and tired-looking man. He carried himself with the air of someone who did physical work, with a walk that spoke of strength and power. But his face and shoulders lacked the same energy.

He looked like the kind of man who had been striking once, but any vibrancy had been replaced by weary resignation that he tried to hide behind a practiced facade. It wasn't hard to recognize the familiar duality of someone pretending at life, the too-wide smile and the fast-but-weary strides. *Single parent*, she assessed perhaps too quickly. *Dad who has to try hard.*

Without any ceremony whatsoever, the little girl climbed up onto the red vinyl counter stool next to Lulu and said, "Hi, I'm Carly. We just got here."

"I'm Lulu," Lulu replied. "I live here."

"Lulu," repeated Carly with admiration. "That's a great name."

"Thanks," replied Lulu with a grin. "I like it."

"She also likes strawberry ice cream. What do you like, Carly?" offered Marvin in a congenial tone. Next to Mayor Jean, Marvin was the unofficial ambassador for Matrimony Valley. Everybody loved Marvin, and not just because he served up delicious ice cream. Whenever she felt blue or insufficient or just plain tired, Marvin's compassion and his ice cream were always ready with a spoon and a smile.

"I like chocolate and vanilla and strawberry. In stripes," the little girl replied. "You got any spumoni?" She put an adorable effort into the difficult word.

"Carly's mom was Italian," the man said. Kelly noticed he said "was," not "is," because like most widows, she always noticed when people spoke about their spouses in the past tense. Especially someone her own age. *So maybe more than just a single parent. Maybe a sole surviving parent.* Her heart pinched at the unfair snap judgment she'd made upon his entrance.

"Spumoni, huh?" Marvin bunched his eyebrows as if this required deep concentration. "Can't say I've got anything that fancy. How about I scoop a little bit of each into one dish and you pretend it's spumoni?"

"Oh, I'm great at pretending."

Weren't all little girls? "I'm guessing you're Bruce," Kelly said, rising up off her stool. When his eyebrows rose, she explained. "A tiny town like this can't hold too many unfamiliar fathers with daughters named Carly. I'm Kelly Nelson, the florist for the wedding. Tina asked me to work with you on the boutonnieres for the groomsmen while you were here."

The slightly suspicious look on his face turned into a sort of bafflement. "Oh, yeah. She said something about that, now I remember."

"I have to say," Kelly went on, "you're the first best man who I've ever had get assigned to pick those out."

Bruce shrugged. "Well, this wedding's unusual in a lot of ways if you ask me. Darren's like a brother to me, but the guy is…weird."

"You're the reindeer wedding!" Lulu exclaimed to her new companions.

"Um, elk, yes," Bruce replied, stuffing his hands in his pockets.

"An elk-themed wedding is an especially… unique choice." Glad she'd happened to bring her tote bag along that had her tablet inside, Kelly grabbed it and nodded toward the small table a few feet away. "Pick out a flavor from Marvin, and why don't we get those boutonnieres picked out right now while the girls are getting friendly?"

As Bruce ordered his sundae from Marvin and made a fuss over his daughter's improvised "spumoni," Kelly began pulling up the photos and notes for the upcoming wedding.

"Tina certainly does believe in group efforts," she said as Bruce sat down. "I've dealt with her for her bouquet, the maid of honor for the attendants' bouquets, Darren's mother for the church decorations and Tina's mom for the reception centerpieces. This is 'wedding by committee' if ever I've seen it."

"That's a nice way to put it," he said, rolling his eyes. "I'd categorize it closer to cat-herding myself. Or is that elk-herding?"

Kelly smiled. "The man clearly loves his work. And I shouldn't laugh. It might be our first elk-themed wedding, but that doesn't mean it'll be the last. We get a lot of tourists up here interested in the elk herd. We owe a lot to our Forest Service guys." After a moment's thought, she added, "Are you one of them?" He had a ranger look about him—rugged and intense—and somewhere in the back of her mind she thought she'd heard Tina mention that all the groomsmen were Darren's Forest Service buddies.

"North Carolina Forest Service helicopter pilot. Based in Kinston. But Carly and I are here early making a vacation out of it."

Kelly tamped down the reaction that still came with the word *pilot*. It wasn't such a tidal wave anymore, mostly just a sharp surge, a "shiver of the soul," as Pastor Mitchell put it. "Fire service?"

"Some," he said. "Mostly support, transportation, supply, that sort of thing. But we do our fair share of fires. Sounds like you've got someone in the service?"

"No," she replied. "My husband was a commercial pilot." *Was, not is.* Did he notice her use of the past tense the way she'd noticed his? It always amazed her how such ordinary words held enough weight to grow a lump in her throat. "But he had friends in the service in Georgia," she added, feeling the past tense of that sentence stick in her throat with the same weight.

The look in his eyes and the pause before his

next question told her he had indeed noticed which tense she'd used. "Retired?" He said it with the low and careful tone of someone who knew there was another possible answer.

Kelly lowered her voice. "Fatal crash. Lightning strike. A few years ago."

He looked down at the table and dragged the next words out in a low voice. "I'm sorry. We…um…we lost Carly's mom Christmas before last. Cancer."

Christmas without the one you love. Was there a bigger hole in the world than trying to survive a child's mourning at Christmastime with your heart in splinters? "I'm so sorry." Funny how they instinctively traded those words that never, ever felt like enough to contain the mountain of pain.

For a moment, neither of them spoke. They both sat up a bit as Marvin set a sizable sundae down next to the peach milkshake she'd brought over from the counter. "Enjoy," Marvin said with his congenial smile. "Welcome to Matrimony Valley."

"Thanks," Bruce replied, looking up with an expertly applied smile Kelly knew all too well. The smile left as Marvin turned away, and for a moment or two Bruce swirled his spoon in the sundae's whipped cream. "It's hard," he said softly, his voice catching a bit on the words. He nodded back in the direction of his daughter. "But I try, you know?"

"I do know. And then there are happy things like Darren and Tina's wedding." She hoped he caught the brightness in her voice. Weddings could be both lovely and excruciating from the viewpoint of a surviving spouse. Watching someone else's heart find happiness always proved a mixed sort of joy.

"Weird, happy things," he amended, a bit of a smile returning to his face. "Tell me you've got some idea for whatever it is I'm supposed to pick, because I sure don't know. Couldn't they have stuck me with just planning the bachelor night like a normal best man?"

"We'll get you through this." Kelly turned the tablet to face him. "Since the groomsmen are all wearing red plaid shirts and gray vests, I thought we'd go with pine and ferns."

He clearly had no preferences. "Looks fine to me. Just nothing fussy."

"Naturally. We'll add a bit of red fabric to match your shirts and the women's boleros."

"Their whats?"

"Boleros," she repeated. "The short jackets made from the same flannel as your shirts that the bridesmaids are wearing over their dresses."

"Boleros, boutonnieres… Why can't they

just call them jackets and flowers? Come to think of it, why do the guys even need flowers anyway?"

So he was going to be one of those, was he? Someone who thought of flowers as expensive and frivolous incidentals, useless details that wilted days after the ceremony? "Every wedding should have beauty and traditions. Since the times of the Greeks and Romans, brides *and* grooms have worn flowers to symbolize hope and new life."

"Fine, if you say so. I just don't get why I'm stuck with choosing this. I mean, Carly could do a better job at this than I could."

Grant me patience, Lord. "Well, then, let's ask her. Carly, Lulu, come tell us what you think."

They gushed over the images on the tablet, of course, because the designs Kelly had created for this event were unique, just like the wedding itself. Samantha Douglas would gush, too, if Kelly had her way. With the girls' help, the boutonnieres were quickly selected.

"All that matters here is that Darren and Tina love the way the ceremony looks and feels," Kelly explained, directing her words at Lulu and Carly since Bruce clearly couldn't care less. "Every detail is a part of that, even the boutonnieres." She turned off the tablet.

"That's how Matrimony Valley works. It's why we do what we do."

Bruce looked at the florist with a foggy sort of awe. How did this Kelly woman pull it off? Here he was, two years out from losing his wife, and he still couldn't manage to feel like much more than the walking wounded. A man in some sort of invisible zombie state, lurching through life, looking alive but feeling half-dead and irreparably damaged every waking moment.

He did *want* to heal. The desire to come back to life still existed somewhere under the mountain of grief. He just didn't know *how* to crawl his way out of this thing that only looked like living. The whole point of taking this time before Darren's wedding was to find a way to snap himself out of this hamster wheel of busy emptiness.

But how? He wanted to be there, *really* be there for Carly, not just running through the parenting paces. He wanted to enjoy this wedding, to be happy for his friend and relish Carly's role in it. Only, in lots of ways he could never admit, the whole thing just bugged him. It hurt. It reminded him of everything he no longer had. Made him so bristly that he took it out on innocent people like this florist, who was only trying to do her job well.

And just to make things worse, this woman seemed to sense the storm of thoughts that had pulled him away from the conversation. "Hey," she said softly. "It gets better."

He merely grunted in reply.

"Not right away," Kelly went on, "and not nearly fast enough, but one day you wake up and you don't feel quite so much like the walking wounded anymore."

It was a shocking sort of comfort that she'd used the very same words that were in his head. "Yeah, everyone keeps saying that."

"Because it's true," she replied. "But you do have to choose it, you know. Walk toward it. Crawl, if you have to."

He ran a hand over his chin. "Not doing so good at that, actually." He wasn't so sure he liked how this woman he didn't really know pulled such huge things out of him. She was prying open boxes. Private boxes he didn't want to open for a very long time, if ever. She looked pushy, too, like the kind of woman who didn't stop when she met resistance.

Kelly straightened, putting her tablet back into the tote bag with a matter-of-fact air. "So, what are your plans for while you're here in the valley?"

"Oh, I've got a lot of things planned. Hikes, trips into Asheville, exploring the falls, looking for wildlife, maybe some sledding if we get any snow. I definitely plan for us to stay busy."

"Busy," she said. He didn't like the way she said it.

"Hey, busy's good. Little girls need to stay busy, right?"

"Sure," she said, but again with a tone that he couldn't quite call agreement. "There's happy, too, you know."

Happy? Come on, happy wasn't really on the table for him at the moment. And he certainly wasn't interested in discussing happiness or its lack in his life with this pushy florist he'd known for fifteen minutes. "Yeah, not so much, lately, if you know what I mean." She did know what he meant, right? She'd been through it.

"So there's nothing that makes you happy?"

My wife is dead. What do you think? "Carly." When she leveled a look at him, he added, "Not much else." Granted, it was a pouty answer, but Bruce wasn't volunteering to become anyone's healing project, not on vacation, or ever.

"Okay," she said slowly in a "so that's

how you want to play it" tone. "What makes Carly happy?"

"Unicorns."

Bruce was just the tiniest bit pleased to have surprised her with the answer. "Unicorns?" she asked.

"Long story I'm not going to tell you."

"Okay," she replied in the same tone as before. "Unicorns and…?" She whirled her hand, as if cuing a list from him.

"Well, based on our day so far, not hikes or wildlife or waterfalls or sledding or anything outdoors." In fact, she'd shut down nearly every suggestion he'd had since they arrived. Except for going for ice cream, and look where *that* had gotten him.

"So what does Carly like?"

She enunciated the words as if he hadn't heard the question the first time. His urge to up and leave was squelched only by the gleeful conversation Carly was having over at the counter with Lulu. He couldn't afford to annoy Lulu's mom if Carly was having so much fun with her daughter, could he? "Pink," he replied, tamping down his irritation. "Spumoni ice cream. Stickers and coloring books. Kittens. Artsy stuff like beads and those rubber loopy bracelet things."

Kelly actually nodded after each of those,

so maybe Carly's favorite things were normal despite how foreign girlie arts and crafts felt to him. "And hopscotch," he went on. It was a wonder he hadn't listed hopscotch first—the game had saved his life so many dreary afternoons. It was mindless motion. You didn't have to think or talk playing hopscotch. Bruce had a roll of painter's tape in his suitcase just so they could put a hopscotch outline on their hotel room carpet if they felt like it.

"Mom?" Kelly's daughter called from the counter.

"Yes, honey?"

"Can Carly come over and play tomorrow after church?"

Kelly actually smiled as if she'd seen that coming a mile off when it had never occurred to him until this moment that Carly could have playdates while on vacation. "Hey, Lulu," Kelly said, raising one knowing eyebrow to him, "you know how to play hopscotch, don't you?"

Lulu spun around on the stool and rolled her eyes. "Of course. *Everybody* knows how to play hopscotch."

"I love hopscotch," Carly gushed. He was cornered now, and he could tell Kelly knew it.

"Pleeeeaaassseee?" both girls pleaded in a

singsong chorus Bruce knew wouldn't let up until he agreed.

"I'd never hear the end of it if I said no," he admitted. "So sure, why not?"

"Hey, can Carly and her dad come to church with us? We're frosting Valentine's cookies at activity time. Miss Yvonne told me."

"Sometimes being friends with the town baker gets you inside information," Kelly remarked with a grin. "Are you and Carly a churchgoing family?"

Though he found the question a bit intrusive, Bruce appreciated that she referred to Carly and him as a family. They still were, if barely, but he'd noticed that people stopped using the noun once Sandy had passed, and that always bugged him. "We used to be."

She didn't reply, but gave him the politely disappointed look he'd gotten from far too many members of the church he and Sandy used to attend. This woman was clearly pushy about more than just flowers.

"Do you always evangelize people who've been in town less than half a day?" It came out sharper than it ought to have, but making peace with the God who'd let Sandy die was a mighty sore subject. People back in Kinston were so cloying about the way they tried to coax him back to church. Rather than supportive, Bruce found the sad sympathy and the trite assurances that Sandy was in "a better place" to be suffocating.

"Hey," she countered, "my daughter's just inviting your daughter to something she thinks is fun. No agenda, no pressure. Just cookies."

Bruce put a hand up. "I admit, I'm a bit… defensive on the subject."

She cracked a smile and raised an eyebrow. "Really? I hadn't noticed."

He dug into his sundae for a moment, not sure how to smooth over the moment or even sure he wanted to.

"I get it," she said after a moment. "Everyone's got an opinion on how you should behave, how you should heal, all that. Most people are trying to be helpful, but not always succeeding."

"No, not always." *Hardly ever.*

Kelly finished her milkshake with a long slurp. "Well, the offer stands. Church is at ten, just down that way." She pointed down the street, and he could see a quaint white steeple sticking up from a line of trees. "Hopscotch begins at…let's say one o'clock. Meet us at the flower shop just next door and we'll walk to my house." She looked up at the sky. "Tina and Darren wanted snow for the wedding. I think they're going to get some."

Bruce had seen the forecast for the coming weekend. "Maybe more than some, huh?"

Kelly's face dropped. "Let's hope not. Three or four inches of pretty fluffy snow is great—this place looks like a wonderland in a fresh snowfall. But a big storm…" She sighed, peering at the sky again. "Right now they're saying the storm will stay west of us. But I expect I don't need to tell a pilot that a million things could happen between now and Thursday when everyone's arriving." She stood and collected her bag. "You may be grateful you came in so early."

"Surely you all are used to substantial snowfalls. I mean, there's a ski resort two towns over." It shouldn't be like his friends in Atlanta who could be blindsided by a snowstorm because they lacked the experience and equipment to deal with the snow-slicked roads and poor visibility.

"We know what to do with snow," she defended. "But when you add planes, deliveries, rental cars, travelers and nervous brides into the mix, you can imagine it gets a bit trickier. Your friend's happiness aside, the valley's got a lot riding on this wedding. I'd rather not have to pull it off in crisis-management mode."

Tina had said something about this place being relatively new at the wedding thing, but Bruce got the sense her tension came from a bit more than that. Her desire to make sure things went well stretched beyond integrity into something that smacked of seriously high stakes. There seemed to be more to this wedding than just a bride and groom saying "I do."

Chapter Three

Jean Tyler clutched her ginger ale and gaped at Kelly. "Really? He used the word *evangelize*?"

Kelly recalled Bruce's sharp look. "Clearly I struck a nerve. I mean, I wouldn't have extended the invitation for them to come to church, but it was Lulu inviting Carly. The two girls hit it off instantly." Back when both women were single moms, coffee before church was a Sunday tradition for Kelly and Jean. Kelly resurrected the tradition before today's service to talk over yesterday's baffling events with the best man and his daughter the flower girl.

"I wish I could be there to see if he shows." Matrimony Valley's pale mayor leaned back in her chair. "I wish I could be anywhere without feeling like I need an airsickness bag in my pocket." She looked down at her bandaged ankle propped up on an ottoman. "I never thought I'd be thankful for a sprained ankle or miss being able to take painkillers so much."

"So no one has figured out the real reason why you fainted on the town hall steps?" Kelly asked.

"I think Yvonne suspects. But you're the only one who knows I'm pregnant. It's far too early to make it public. But I was never this sick with Jonah. Well, not with morning sickness." Jean's young son, Jonah, was deaf as a result of a severe fever Jean had contracted while pregnant. Kelly understood why it made her friend skittish about this new baby on the way, despite how blissfully happy Jean was now that she'd reconciled with and married Josh—Jonah's father. "How's the wedding going? I'm thrilled you got Samantha Douglas. Coverage from *Southeastern Nuptials* could make a huge difference for us."

"I sure hope so. George is threatening to go on the fritz again, and I hate having to say a prayer every time I turn ignition on the van." Kelly looked up at this morning's sunnier skies. "The spring brides can't get here soon enough. The snow, on the other hand, can take its sweet time."

"Oh, I know. Josh has been watching the weather reports, too. He's trying to get out to San Jose and back one more time next week." Josh and a partner ran a successful software company on the West Coast. While he'd arranged to live here most of the time, work still involved many trips to California. "The last thing I need is for him to be snowbound somewhere in Tennessee with me like this." She put one hand on her belly and gingerly wiggled the toes that poked out from the bandage.

Kelly squeezed Jean's hand. "Come on, you know Josh. He'd buy a snowmobile and plow his way over the mountains to get to your side if you needed him." She returned her gaze upward. There was almost a whole week until the wedding, and mountain weather was nothing if not changeable. Today's sunshine could easily flee and be replaced by clouds dumping a load of snow into Matrimony Valley. "I'd hate for weather to complicate things for the wedding, that's for sure."

"There is always that for winter weddings, isn't there?" Jean patted her stomach. "The upcoming attraction here and I picked the wrong wedding to stick you with."

Kelly didn't want her friend worrying like that. "Hey, every wedding is complicated in its own way. Believe it or not, this couple seems very easygoing. Well, except for the best man, that is."

"You're right—he doesn't sound easygoing at all," Jean agreed.

"The challenges are all logistical. And those are always easier than the emotional ones, you know that." She dunked the doughnut from Yvonne Niles's Bliss Bakery into the steaming cup of coffee Josh had offered her when she'd arrived. They used to do these gatherings outside so that Jonah and Lulu could play before church, but now Josh could be outside with the children while she sat warm and cozy in Jean's living room.

Jean set down her ginger ale. "So, how many contingency plans do you have?"

"Two," Kelly replied, gaining a suspicious look from the friend who knew her too well. "Well, okay, maybe four."

Jean settled back and crossed her arms over her chest. "Well, let's hear 'em." While Jean had often chided Kelly for her controlling tendencies, it had always been a warmhearted, good-natured teasing rather than any kind of reproach. And she was always willing to listen to Kelly's ideas and plans—the ones that let her feel a little more control over all the potential problems in her path.

"If a storm socks in the Asheville airport,

Tina and her parents can divert to Charlotte and we can send someone with a truck to pick them up. Hailey's got a 'snowbound special' all set up to let guests have extra nights at the inn for a discounted price so they won't feel compelled to leave right away if the roads are bad. Rob Folston's stocked up on supplies at the hardware store, and Bill Williams said he'd lend out skates and flood the yard in the back of the store to make an impromptu ice rink to entertain stranded guests."

"All very clever," Jean said.

"And I convinced Samantha Douglas to come up for a set of exclusive interviews on Thursday so she'll already be here before the worst of the storm is scheduled to hit—if it hits at all."

"Brilliant!" exclaimed Jean. "What interviews?"

"Well," Kelly admitted, "I don't exactly have those arranged yet. Both Darren and Tina are supposed to arrive that day, so I'm planning both of them if they'd be willing. And... I was hoping a certain mayor would consent to one."

"Gladly." Jean smiled. "But it'll need to be a house call." She wiggled her toes again, then winced. "Ouch. I really do miss those pain meds. Between my ankle and my stomach, this baby's going to owe me."

Kelly opted to shift the conversation away from wedding contingency plans. The last thing Jean needed was additional stress. "Any chance you can make it to the church's Valentine's Day party?"

"I hope so." Jean shifted in her seat. "I can't just disappear—I've got to show up a few places around town. I'll just be munching on soda crackers rather than any chocolate and cookies." The mother-to-be sighed. "I miss real food. I've been living on crackers, soup, ginger ale and toast. I'm jealous of your doughnut," she whined. "I'm jealous of Jonah's peanut butter and jelly, and I don't even like peanut butter."

Kelly checked her watch; it was nice to catch up with her friend, but she needed to get going. She ought to be at church early on the off chance prickly Bruce Lohan actually did accept Lulu's invitation. "Hang in there, Jean. This can't last long. And just think how thrilled everyone will be when you can announce the baby. Josh looks over the moon as it is—I don't think this will stay secret for long."

"My head knows that. My stomach, not so much." Jean managed a pale smile as she shifted in her seat. "Just keep us in your prayers, okay?"

"You know I will. You sit tight and try not to worry. I've got everything for this wedding under control." Kelly gently hugged her friend. "Tina and Darren will have a terrific event, and Samantha Douglas will run out of superlatives to use in her article. We'll have next winter booked solid with weddings before the Fourth of July."

As she and Lulu walked the few blocks toward church with Jonah and Josh, Kelly took stock of all the businesses along the avenue. Bill Williams, who ran the Catch Your Match Outfitters with his wife, Rose, could handle the slow winters. They ran full tilt during the summer not only with wedding guests but with locals who needed to stock up on gear for fishing trips. Wanda and Wayne Watson's diner never really ebbed or flowed with wedding traffic, but they had seen an uptick in business despite Wanda's rampant skepticism at the Matrimony Valley idea at first. The diner had been and would always be the place where locals ate—that would never change. Yvonne Niles's bakery, like Kelly's flower shop, had the most to gain from weddings. And both women were eager to see their businesses expand.

A fully booked year—think of what that could do for the valley! Weddings were a months-ahead kind of business. A fully booked year would take away so much of the guessing and doubts of her life. With the exception of a few reliable holidays like Valentine's Day, Easter, Christmas and such, flowers were mostly an impulse purchase, or bought for occasions such as birthdays or anniversaries that were significant only to a single couple—making a single purchase—at a time. A steadily predictable wedding income could mean the world to her and Lulu.

Kelly looked up at the clear winter sky and its assortment of fluffy clouds. *You've taken enough from me, Mother Nature*, she chided silently. *Time to cut me a break and just send a pretty dusting of snow. No storm, you hear? The elk wedding needs to be perfect.*

Bruce tried again. "I bet the woods look beautiful this morning. Chock-full of unicorns. Waffles, and then a walk—what do you say?"

Carly flopped over on her bed like a five-year-old heap of drama. "I wanna go to Lulu's church and make Valentine's cookies."

The Almighty wasn't fighting fair, bringing frosting into this. "You have to sit still a lot

during church. Do you remember?" The fact
that he had to ask pinched at his conscience.

"I can sit still just fine. I wanna go. Lulu
says it's lots of fun."

For you, maybe, he thought, trying to en-
vision himself sitting in a church pew again.

"We won't know anybody there except
Kelly and Lulu." Even as the words left his
mouth, they felt like a weak argument. Besides, if almost no one knew him, then maybe
no one could do that super-supportive "we
want to be here for you" thing that made him
cringe.

He looked at Carly's pleading eyes, aware
he was losing this argument. Bruce Lohan
had delivered firefighters into blazing moun-
tainsides and pulled rescue victims from rag-
ing waters, but evidently he was no match for
his daughter's pout, or God wielding cookies.

And so it wasn't that much of a surprise that
at 9:50 a.m. Bruce found himself standing at
the door of Matrimony Valley Community
Church, dragging his feet up the steps behind
Carly's insistent pulling.

"Carly!" Lulu greeted happily as they hung
their coats on the set of racks just inside the
door. "Come sit with us!"

"Oh, I don't know," Kelly said, clearly giving Bruce an out if he wanted one.

Bruce actually couldn't decide which was worse—sitting with Kelly and Lulu or enduring the church service alone. He'd gone to a handful of services after Sandy's passing, and once Carly skipped off to children's church he'd felt excruciatingly solitary sitting in the pew alone.

Carly decided for him. "I do. C'mon, Dad." And with that, she trotted off into the sanctuary holding hands with Lulu as if it were the easiest thing in the world. His daughter had no idea that just walking into the space set a lump of ice into Bruce's gut that threatened to send him running for the door.

"We don't bite," Kelly said. "Well, except maybe cookies."

"Ha," he said drily, too tense to appreciate the attempt at humor.

"Consider it a test run for the wedding, then," she said, starting to follow the girls to a pew that was way too close to the front for his taste. He'd have preferred the far corner of the last pew, but it wasn't going to happen. "This way, the ceremony won't be your first time in here. Familiar spaces are always easier, and the day will be tough enough already."

At least Kelly got how hard this wedding was going to be for him. Other people got it, sort of, but Bruce knew they couldn't really understand the painful happiness Tina and Darren's wedding represented for him. Everyone else was caught up—and rightly so—in the happiness that weddings ought to be. He'd been ecstatic on his wedding day, still a tiny bit unbelieving that he'd landed this beauty who seemed so far out of his league. Stunned that the woman who'd left him dumbstruck at their first meeting had actually fallen for the likes of him, just a normal guy.

A normal guy. Funny how "normal" looked so appealing. Something still beyond his reach. And yet, without the weight of his history driving people to smother him with concern, he could almost feel something close to normal here.

Why? Because it was different? Free from the soaking of memory that usually caught him up short? He'd tried to return to church back in Kinston, he really had. But the place just could never be anything but where they held Sandy's funeral. Kelly talked as if she drew hope and encouragement from her church, but he wasn't there yet. He wondered if he ever would be again.

Bruce took his seat in the small pew, he and Kelly flanking the girls on either side. He tried to discount the weirdly family-ish feeling sitting in a pew with these three people gave him, finding it ridiculous. He'd known two of them for one day. Just because Carly made instant friendships didn't mean he had to. Be nice, yes, but get close? No.

Rather than look in Kelly's direction, Bruce scanned the small sanctuary. Maybe his strange sense of comfort came from the fact that this place looked nothing like the large and fancy church back home. It was a bright and simple space. Peaceful. With the character that came from years and history. Neat but not fancy. Perfect for the kind of wedding Tina and Darren wanted.

Not that sitting here was effortless. More than once one of them had to "shush" the excited girls. Kids were such naturals at instant friendships. Carly's smiles and stifled giggles were worth a prickly hour in a strange sanctuary, weren't they?

Except sitting through the service didn't actually feel that strange. Did he still have a bone to pick with the Almighty? Sure, that wasn't going to disappear after the mountain of pain he'd been climbing over the past two years. But church itself? Church was different from God, even though he couldn't quite say why. Church was people. Back home in Kinston, it was nosy, prodding, pitying people with concerned faces and endless hugs. People who said "How are you?" with such an invasive persistence. Church with a bunch of people he didn't know ended up a lot easier than church with all those he did. The unfamiliarity gave him space to just be, somehow. Was it a deep, spiritual experience? No. But it wasn't nearly as awful as he'd expected it to be.

Sure, it felt awkward when Carly and Lulu raced off down the hallway with the other children, leaving a gaping space in the pew he and Kelly occupied. He watched Kelly fidget and take pains not to look his way, so he knew she felt it, as well. An uncomfortable awareness threatened to distract him from the service, and he fought to keep his attention on Pastor Mitchell's message about the true nature of love.

He was relieved no one quoted the "love is patient, love is kind" verse Sandy's sister had read at their wedding. The message instead focused on the strength love brought to the world. How love stood up against the darkness with God's relentless care for His people. How love transformed and redeemed. How God's love could do things that human love so often failed to do: find the good, grow the hope, see the true value. He liked the pastor's idea that love was a constant outside of human relationships. It helped him think there could and would be love left in the world despite the huge chunk of it that had been ripped from his life. Maybe he wasn't ready to see that love now, but perhaps he could again someday.

"The best thing about God's love is that you don't have to reach for it," Pastor Mitchell said. "It reaches for you. Sometimes even before you want it or feel ready for it. Wherever you go, there it is. All God asks of you is to turn and see it. Let it in."

People were always quick to tell him what he needed to do to move on. Join this support group, read this book, do this, stop doing that. Mitchell's sermon was the first message he'd heard that told him to just be, and maybe crack himself the tiniest bit open. Maybe struggling to escape the fog wasn't the answer. Maybe he just had to wait for the fog to lift on its own.

And wasn't that an uncomfortable notion. Waiting? Getting—what had the pastor called it—expectantly still? The very thought made every inch of his insides itch.

When the girls returned for the final hymn, each bearing a generously frosted giant heart cookie wrapped in pink sparkly cellophane, Bruce couldn't decide if he wanted to stick around or run.

The girls, of course, were busy making

plans to spend the entire day together. "Can Lulu come to lunch with us?" Carly asked.

"Well, now…" he hedged, not wanting to be rude, but needing some space after the jumble of his reactions this morning.

Clearly he hadn't hid it well, because Kelly stepped in. "The grown-ups decided we'd each do lunch on our own."

They hadn't, of course, but he was grateful for the out she gave him. "You just spent a whole hour with each other. I think you can live through being separated for lunch."

A chorus of little-girl moans erupted until Kelly held both hands up. "Enough of that. Carly, we'll see you at one o'clock." She turned to Bruce. "Thank you for coming to church with us. I hope you got something out of it."

He did—he just couldn't exactly say what.

Chapter Four

"Do you think Carly and Mr. Bruce liked our church, Mom?" Lulu asked as they loaded the dishwasher from Sunday lunch.

"I can't say for sure, sweetheart." She'd been surprised that Bruce and Carly had shown for church, but he'd looked unsettled during most of the service, and hadn't spoken much afterward.

The man was impossible to read. Had he been irritated by the country congregation, or just needed some time to process his reaction?

"Carly's fun. I really like her."

I can't really say the same for her father, Kelly thought. "She seems like a nice friend to have." She handed a glass to Lulu.

"Carly said our church is tons more fun than the one she used to go to when her mom was alive."

Kelly felt her heart pinch the way it always did when young Lulu talked about a parent dying in such a matter-of-fact way. It shouldn't ever be normal, not to any child. And yet Carly's remark told her a lot about Bruce, didn't it? He'd been part of a church community, and then cut himself off—for whatever reason—after his wife's death.

Why? Kelly couldn't imagine how she'd have gotten through the dark days after Mark's death without the support of MVCC. The congregation had held her up, prayed her through, even fed her. Though her own parents were far away in Texas, she'd never been alone, but had multiple invitations to choose from on those crushing first holidays and birthdays. How could anyone do it alone like he seemed to have? She wondered if the bruised nature of his soul—and he surely appeared to be a wounded soul to her—had come from that isolation. It made her sad and wary at the same time. Whatever small connection she felt with the man or his adorable daughter had to be tempered by the fact that he was a long way from healing.

"How much longer till they get here?" Lulu whined.

"Oh, just enough time for you to get your

math worksheet done," Kelly said, pointing to Lulu's backpack on its hook by the door.

"Mom, it's Sunday. Pastor says it's rest day," Lulu retorted, one cocky hand on her slim hips.

"Then maybe you'll need a nap to pass the time," Kelly teased.

Lulu rolled her eyes. "Fine. Math is better than naps. But not by much." She pulled a folder out of her backpack and flopped down on the kitchen counter with a dramatic sigh. "Third grade is hard."

Thirty-one is harder, Kelly moaned in the silence of her heart. And lately, for a host of reasons, thirty-one alone felt extra hard.

When the doorbell rang twenty minutes later, Lulu scampered off her seat and made it to the door before Kelly even put down the magazine she was reading.

"It took *forever*!" Carly announced once Lulu mentioned how long the wait had seemed.

Kelly gave a soft laugh at the girls' enthusiasm. "Remember when two hours was forever?" she asked Bruce.

"Not really," Bruce replied, scratching his chin.

"Wouldn't it be great if we got a snow day this week that closed school so you could come over again?" Lulu said as she opened the hall cabinet where the driveway chalk was kept.

"Are we gonna get lots of snow, Daddy? You said Miss Tina wanted to be a snow bride." Carly clearly thought lots of snow sounded like a marvelous idea.

"Then I'd like four inches, please," Kelly offered. "Fluffy not icy, with a nice, quiet wind. And sunshine by ten in the morning on the wedding day."

Bruce furrowed his brow. "Not too particular, are you?"

Kelly gestured out the window. "We look gorgeous in a few inches of snow and bright sunshine. Like a postcard."

"What about all of Miss Tina's pretty flowers? Won't they freeze?" The little girl's concern was touching.

"No," Kelly assured her. "I made sure to use flowers just right for a winter's day." Kelly was especially proud of the creative mix of winter-hardy amaryllis, anemones and silver brunia balls she'd designed, perfectly accented with pine and red ribbons. Like the cake Yvonne had designed, Kelly was sure nothing matched it anywhere in Asheville.

"Here's the chalk for hopscotch," Lulu pronounced, holding up the bucket. Obviously, there was not a minute to waste.

"Hat," Kelly reminded Lulu.

"And mittens," Bruce chimed in, for Carly had a hood on her sweet pink-and-purple jacket.

"Mom," Lulu moaned, followed by a copy-cat "Dad" from Carly, though both girls obeyed the instructions.

They watched the girls race out the side door without so much as a single look back.

"I feel bad adding to your load on a Sunday…" Bruce began.

"Oh, no," she cut in, "you're actually help-ing. Keeping Lulu occupied can be a bit of a challenge sometimes." Kelly caught the mix of relief and reluctance in Bruce's eyes. Was he glad that Carly was so excited to play or sorry she'd left him so eagerly while they were supposed to be on vacation together? *All of the above*, she thought to herself. *Every single parent knows that mix.* "I can call you at the inn when they finally wear out, or—" it might be nice to grab an hour of productive solitude while the girls played, but she also had something particular she wanted to ask Bruce about "—I can make some coffee. I'm a big fan of afternoon coffee."

She was surprised when he said, "Coffee

sounds great, thanks." Maybe he didn't quite know what he'd do with himself while Carly was occupied. While part of her envied that kind of space in his life—the room to take a vacation without worrying over a million details connected to her job—she also remembered feeling like she'd never fill the lonely hours of her long days in that first year with Mark gone.

Kelly waited until they'd settled at the kitchen island, watching the girls draw and play a round of hopscotch, before she said, "Carly said something to Lulu at church this morning. About the unicorns."

His look told her he didn't really want to cover this topic.

She pursued it anyway. "She told Lulu her mother sends the unicorns, and she asked Lulu why they didn't have any in the valley."

Bruce rubbed the back of his neck and set down the coffee mug. "I don't know where this unicorn business came from. She started talking about them the day before Sandy died, when we knew it would be any moment. She was looking out the window as we were getting ready to go to the hospice center and all of a sudden she looks at me and says, 'Mom's friend the unicorn is in the woods behind the house.' Just like that. Like there was nothing unusual about it." He sighed. "I played along. I mean, what else could I do in all that sadness?"

"That's not a bad thing," she offered, hoping to soothe the dismay still lingering in his eyes at the memory.

"That's what I thought, but then one came—or at least, Carly said one came—every day after that. Her eyes sort of lit up when she told me. I figured it was something she…needed somehow. I mean, for weeks I thought I heard Sandy's voice in the hallway or saw her out of the corner of my eye after she was…gone. I figured this was the same thing." He looked down at his coffee. "The child grief counselor didn't seem to be worried, and I was barely holding it together as it was—I was in no shape to lecture Carly about the dangers of counting on unicorns." A heartbreaking worry filled Bruce's expression. "But now that's coming back to haunt me, since she hasn't seen them lately."

"I'm not a grief counselor—a survivor maybe," Kelly replied, "but from what I can tell, she seems to be coping okay to me." She glanced out the window where the girls were having a grand time. "There's still lots of joy in her." She decided to go out on a limb. "You, on the other hand, look pretty wrung out."

He shifted his weight and shook his head. "Nah, I'm okay."

Kelly offered a smile. "I used to say that all the time, too. Long before it was even close to true. Everybody thinks I'm coping great—and most days I am—but there are still days…" She knew she didn't have to finish the thought.

"Lulu's been so nice to Carly. Your daughter's a great kid."

Now, there was something a struggling single parent couldn't hear often enough. "Thanks."

"How old was she when your husband died?"

"Six."

Bruce swallowed hard. "Carly was only three when Sandy died. Does Lulu remember her dad?"

Kelly's heart twisted. Wasn't that the crux of it for everyone in their shoes? "Yes," she reassured him. "I make sure she does."

He could make sure Carly remembered Sandy. The need to do that drummed like a pulse through him every single day. He was glad to hear of Kelly's success on that front, but it still bugged him that conversations with Kelly Nelson always went places he didn't want to go. He would have been better off reading a book in his hotel room instead of sitting here asking questions he shouldn't and having answers pulled out of him he didn't want to divulge. Why was she able to get things out of him like this? And why had he let her drag him back to church, for crying out loud?

He hadn't really minded church as much as he thought he would, but he sure wasn't going to mention that in front of Kelly. At this rate, she'd probably have him attending potlucks or some widowers' Bible study by Friday.

He didn't live here; he was just a visitor. So why were she and Lulu so bent on making him and Carly feel welcome? Was that a valley thing? A wedding thing? Or just a Nelson family thing?

One half of him didn't want to keep talking to her, but the other half of him was desperate to know how she pulled off the control she seemed to have. The control he couldn't seem to find. "When'd you get your balance back?" he blurted out after a short pause in conversation. His life felt like a bicycle most days—living a crazy need to keep pedaling so he didn't tip over.

She gave a quiet laugh. "You're assuming I had any in the first place."

"You've got more than I can manage at the

moment. I don't know how much more scrambling I've got left in me, you know?" He shook his head. "That's a stupid thing to say." The gentle recognition he saw in her eyes kept making him blurt things out.

"Oh, no, I get it. Busy feels good—well, better than the alternative, at least. Some days I wonder if there'll ever be enough of me to make a decent life for Lulu and me. I mean, running the flower shop in a tiny town—even a tiny wedding town—isn't exactly a sure-fire plan for solid success. Well-adjusted people don't lie awake at night wondering how much longer a flower cooler named George will hang on."

Lie awake at night wondering how many more days. Isn't that exactly what he'd done on Sandy's last days? Terrified to fall asleep for fear he'd miss the moment she slipped away from him?

Kelly looked up at the ceiling. "Now who's saying stupid things? That was insensitive, to say the least."

"No," he said. "Kind of feels better to be able to say it. People are always so careful around me. I don't want to be this fragile. I'm tired of being less than okay, on the verge of okay, anything but okay. Only I don't know how to get to okay from here." He looked over to see Carly looking into the kitchen window, waving to him with a happy, floppy mitten. "How to get *her* to okay. I mean, the whole unicorn thing. Either she isn't seeing them, and she's upset, or she *is* seeing them—which means she's living in a fantasy instead of reality. That can't be okay."

"For her, maybe it is. I still get near hysterical on an airplane." She sighed. "I don't think there are rules to this. Not with kids, not with us." She paused for a moment before saying, "I think maybe one of the reasons Lulu is so taken with Carly is that they've both lost someone. Lulu has friends who have single parents from divorce, but Carly is the first person in her age group Lulu knows who's had a parent die." She squinted her eyes shut. "I hate that verb, you know. 'Die.' 'Passed' sounds like it isn't enough, and 'die' sounds like it's too much."

Bruce nodded his agreement. He hated most of the words associated with what happened. *Deceased. Lost her battle to cancer. Widower. Bereaved.* None of the language ever came close to describing the thing anyway.

"Have you had friends do the pushy date thing?" he asked, just to change the subject.

That brought a real, full laugh from her. "Oh, yes. And believe me, there aren't a lot of eligible bachelors my age in a place like this. Plus—no offense to your gender—having a child in tow doesn't exactly light up your prospects with most guys." She looked at him. "You'll have it easier, though. It may be a gross generalization, but I think women take to blending families easier than men do."

He couldn't believe he was asking. "But you're looking?"

She shook her head. "Not really. I don't know about you, but what I had with Mark was better than lots of thirty-year marriages I've seen. Absolutely too short, but oh, it was terrific. I hit the jackpot on the first time out. Trying again just feels like inviting disappointment." She pulled in a deep breath. "No, I'd rather spend my time helping other people get married."

Kelly sounded so content, so in control. She'd made peace with the parts of her life that had been taken away. She had plans and goals, wasn't lurching though life in survival mode, doing the bare minimum to get by. Was it the constancy of her faith that had done that? His own faith had seemed to evaporate into a thin film of anger for him on the day of Sandy's funeral. Was she just better suited to this survival journey than he was? Or was it just that time healed like everyone said?

Maybe it really was time. He could almost believe, listening to her, that he could get to where she was one day. Right now, he just needed to get through the upcoming wedding, and maybe it wasn't the worst thing in the world if she helped a bit with that.

Chapter Five

Bruce and Carly managed to have a pleasant "vacation" day Monday. Visiting Darren and his elk herd up at the national park, they'd had a whole long, unhurried day out in nature. Darren's elk had always fascinated Carly; he'd often wondered if they were the source of her imaginary unicorn thing. She'd "seen" one of her unicorns in the forest, playing among the elk herd. Was that good? Or bad? Whatever it was, the sighting had put her in a good mood, which at least meant his plans to spend quality time with Carly might succeed.

Until Tuesday morning anyway. The first words out of his daughter's mouth were a whiny, "I'm tired of outdoor stuff. I wanna go play with Lulu today."

Had anyone ever thought about bottling a five-year-old's bored whine as a deterrent? To anything and everything? He loved Carly, but that girl had a pitch to her whine that could set his teeth on edge. He'd been expecting a request for a repeat visit to Lulu's, but he'd thought it would at least come after breakfast. Not his daughter's first waking words. "Good morning to you, too, sunshine," he said.

"Can I?" She padded over in bright yellow pajamas covered in rainbows.

He put down his newspaper and pulled her up onto his lap. "Lulu has school today, remember? I thought you and I could have fun."

"Is it gonna snow today? Can we go sledding?"

Bruce turned to the weather page at the back of the paper and pointed to the pictures that showed the week's forecast. He pointed to the big snowflake on the box marked for Thursday, the one after the box with the big heart on Wednesday for the holiday. "The snow isn't coming until after Valentine's Day." He noticed, but didn't explain, the warnings about significant snowfall for the weekend. "But there are lots of other fun things we can do before then. We haven't gone to see the bakery, or the fishing store, or visited the frozen waterfall yet."

"Lulu said her favorite bookstore is in the big city nearby. Can we go there today?"

It was starting to feel as if Lulu's and Kelly's suggestions or invitations were scheduling his vacation. Maybe getting out of Matrimony Valley and making the short drive to Asheville was a good idea. He wanted at least one more day with just the two of them, and that might not happen if he stayed in town.

And it might be good to get Carly someplace out of the woods, where he wouldn't be continually watching for her to see unicorns. Because unicorns didn't live in the city, right? If that was how this worked. Truth was, he had no idea how the whole unicorn thing worked, or what it was supposed to accomplish—if it accomplished anything other than making Carly smile. The conversation earlier with Kelly had made him feel slightly better about it, but had brought up a whole bunch of questions, as well.

"Hey, kiddo," he asked, snuggling her close and hoping to effect a change of topic, "do you have any questions about Mr. Darren's wedding? You've got a big role to play, you know."

That perked her up. "Not as big as yours. Will you be really busy being bestest man?"

Bruce found her version of the title heartening. "Bestest" at anything felt far beyond his reach these days. "Not so busy that you can't be my date. And you can stay at the reception as long as you like, even way past your bedtime."

She giggled. "I'm your date. That's funny." She settled in against him, measuring her small hand up against his. He wondered if she thought the space on his ring finger looked as empty as he did, if she had any memory of the rings tucked away in a velvet box at the top of his closet. "Did you and Mom have a flower girl at your wedding?"

He'd been waiting for the impending wedding to bring up her curiosity about his and Sandy's ceremony. But even if this was expected, he still didn't feel prepared. How could he talk about it with the joy and warmth it deserved, not with the huge sense of loss the memories invoked? He put on a smile. "We did. A little girl named Nancy. She stole the show, just like I expect you will. We looked at the pictures, remember?" Carly loved seeing her mother glowing and gowned like a princess. He'd looked at the love in Sandy's eyes in those photographs and felt an ache that took his breath away.

Carly's eyes were so much like Sandy's. He hugged his daughter tight. "It's okay to feel a bit sad about the wedding. It's okay if it makes you miss Mom."

"It kinda does." She looked up at him, and

he thought he saw a bit of relief in her expression. *Finally*, he thought, *I got something right in helping her through this.*

He gave the only answer he could. "Me, too."

"But Lulu doesn't have a daddy anymore. Her mom is like you, and she goes to weddings all the time."

He wasn't quite sure where she was headed with that, but it fascinated him that Lulu and Carly had shared about their missing parents. How did kids open up with no hesitation like that? Then again, hadn't he and Kelly done much the same thing? And yet Bruce couldn't think of an instance before Kelly where he'd shared about Sandy in a first conversation. He used one of Sandy's tricks when Carly said something mystifying: "So…?"

"So it has to be fun. The wedding, I mean. Otherwise why do it?"

Carly had a point. A wedding could be fun. Bittersweet, maybe—especially since this would be the first he'd attended since Sandy's passing—but maybe he could push himself toward looking forward to the happiness of his good friend. "Good point. Hey, what do you say we practice our dancing again before breakfast?"

He pulled her upright and held out his

hands. She stepped gingerly onto his feet and looked up at him with a baffled grin. "We're in our pj's. And there's no music."

"Who cares? We'll make our own. Sing me a song."

Carly launched into a silly number from one of her favorite television shows, and he slowly began to move his feet with hers atop his. He'd been a good dancer—Sandy loved to dance—but the lilting one-two-three of this father-daughter version always felt more like a swaying hug to him. A tiny demonstration that they still constituted a family, broken as they were. She loved it as much as he did. It was one of the few things that still felt as good as it had before Sandy died.

Bruce danced around the room with his daughter, humming along with her, lifting his feet in careful, rhythmic steps and relishing the small weight of her bare feet wiggling on top of his. Something close to joy—like the start of a sunrise or the sparks of a fireplace just catching—pulled at the edges of his numbness. The smile he gave Carly didn't require so much effort; it came up naturally. With ease. How few things came with ease anymore.

He thought about Sandy's love of weddings. He pictured the ruffled red plaid flannel jumper Carly was going to wear in the ceremony with her white tights and little hunting boots—Sandy would have found it adorable. Sandy would have known what to do with Carly's hair for the occasion. As it was, he was stumped. A ponytail was the extent of his skills, and surely this required something a bit fancier. He'd need to ask Kelly or Tina what to do.

"Daddy…" came Carly's voice as her hands squeezed his. "Where'd you go?"

Bruce wanted to kick himself. Even here, now, in this tiny moment of joy, Carly still recognized he wasn't fully present. He hated how she noticed. He should be looking into his daughter's eyes, not thinking about how he could almost feel happy with her dancing on his feet. The whole point of this vacation was to spend time *with* her, not just beside her.

He didn't have an answer to Carly's question. Not one he could explain to a five-year-old, at least. Instead, he hoisted her up and wrapped her in a hug, snuggling his nose into her neck in the way that always sent her into fits of giggles. "You're gonna be so cute at that wedding. I'll be dancing with the prettiest girl in the room."

"Daddy," she admonished with an air of authority, "the *bride* is s'posed to be the prettiest. Everybody's s'posed to be looking at her." She rolled her eyes in a way that made Bruce fearful of her teenage years. "You can't say that in front of Miss Tina."

"Can I say it to you?"

The way she furrowed her brows was all Sandy. "Just here. Not later."

"Okay, then, let's get dressed and get this day started. Asheville's waiting for us."

Indulgences came few and far between in Kelly's life these days, but a really good cup of coffee from the shop near the floral wholesaler in Asheville topped the list.

Superior caffeine was necessary, given how crazy today had been at the wholesale flower market. *Well, tomorrow's Valentine's Day—what did you expect?* At least she'd managed to get most of the hardier wedding greenery today as well, making Friday's wedding run a tiny bit easier. *I might pull off this crazy busy week after all*, she mused.

"Hi!" came a small voice from behind her on the sidewalk.

Kelly turned to see Bruce Lohan and Carly, loaded down with shopping bags. Why was it this man was suddenly everywhere in her life? "Well, hello there," she greeted. "Looks like you two had a fun morning." Yesterday the state park, today Asheville. Other than to get married, most people came to Matrimony Valley to relax. Bruce Lohan's idea of "vacation" certainly was a busy one.

"We went to the bookstore," Carly said, holding up a small bag.

Kelly recognized the logo. "Oh, that's Lulu's favorite."

"And the cupcake shop," Carly added.

Kelly peered at the collection of bags Bruce carried. "And the toy store, and the craft store, and the museum. It's barely lunch—you've been busy." Ah, but five-year-olds could be an energetic lot, couldn't they?

"We haven't had lunch yet," Carly proclaimed. "We just had cupcakes. Hamburgers are next."

There was something to be said for a man who could embrace a dessert-before-lunch mentality. Usually it was grandparents who indulged like that. "What books did you buy?"

Carly set down her bags. "I got two about unicorns." She pulled out a pair of picture books and a small stuffed unicorn with a rainbow hair and tail.

Kelly smiled, remembering how little girls could be with their animal fixations. Lulu obsessed about kittens at Carly's age. Kitten books, kitten sheets, kitten pajamas, stuffed kittens…it was a wonder they had managed to come this far without acquiring a family cat. Yet. She'd heard a rumor about Maureen Rogers's cat getting ready to have kittens—a rumor Lulu had brought up many times.

"Did Dad buy any books?"

Bruce maneuvered his own load of bags to reach into another one from the bookstore. He produced *101 Things to Do with Kids*. She offered him a polite smile. He'd been Carly's father for five years. He ought to be past the deer-in-headlights quality she kept seeing behind his eyes. Didn't he know how to spend time with his child without an instruction manual? *Stop that*, she told herself. *Grief does different things to everybody.*

"So, what brings you down to the city?" he asked as he returned the book to its bag.

"Flowers for Valentine's Day, mostly, but also getting a head start on your friend's wedding. Their style calls for much more greenery than floral, and since that lasts so much longer I can pick up things on this trip and save Friday for the more delicate stems."

Kelly ignored the rusty squeak as she pulled open the van doors. Inside, the cargo area burst to the brim with blooms in red, pink and white along with a generous supply of green boughs. Carly "oohed" as the dual scent of roses and pine wafted out onto the sidewalk.

Bruce let out an impressed whistle. "Going to be a busy week for you, isn't it?"

"Yes, but I always try to remember that busy is good."

"Busy is good, yes—frantic, no. I don't think I ever realized what a double load a just-after-Valentine's-Day wedding was for a florist."

Kelly thought four shops and a museum before lunch was rather frantic, but Carly seemed happy enough. Lulu would have been fussy after a morning that packed at that age. Then again, not everyone gravitated to the slower pace of small-town life, did they? "Maybe a bit frantic. I can't afford to complain when business piles up. I just try to stay grateful—" she held up her cup "—and caffeinated."

Bruce smiled. "I hear you there. Hey, would you like to join us for burgers before we head on to the Biltmore Estate?"

The huge Biltmore Estate? In a short afternoon? With a five-year-old? That took courage…or foolishness. "I can't," she replied. "Gotta get all this back to the shop and get ready for tomorrow." She was going to be working half the night at the shop as it was—lunch would be little more than the yogurt and crackers from home sitting in the shop cooler. The coffee in her hands had been her single splurge for the day.

"Can Lulu and I play together tomorrow?" Carly asked.

"We might be able to work something out," Kelly offered. The little girl really was sweet, and Lulu seemed to adore her.

"I like Lulu."

"I know you do, sweetheart," Bruce replied. "But remember, everybody's got a big week ahead."

True enough. Kelly waved as she shut the van doors. "We'll see how it goes, okay? Have fun, you two."

"We will!" Carly called as the two of them set off down the street.

Kelly smiled, remembering Bruce's activity book. Her version would read, *101 Things I Have to Do before Tomorrow.* Two months back, Lulu had asked to go to the special Christmas events at the Biltmore, but Kelly had never managed to find the time. And a vacation? She hadn't taken one since Mark had died. *What would I do with that kind of time?* she wondered.

If this feature in Southeastern Nuptials *does what I hope, I'll finally get the chance to find out.* To be able to hire a second full-time person in the shop would be such a luxury. Lulu loved the shop, and was great about spending afternoons there and evenings when needed, but Kelly wanted to do better by her girl. She wanted to do better for herself, to stop feeling the constant pressure of making ends meet. To get to a place where a surprise like van repairs or a doctor's visit for Lulu didn't feel capable of pulling her under.

As she got in the van, Kelly caught her reflection in the rearview mirror. *I look tired. I am tired. But that's okay, I can deal with tired. I'm finally getting ahead, things are finally starting to feel solid.* She just had to hold out till the June weddings pushed things over the top.

Until then, it was Valentine's Day and elks and flannel and coffee.

Lots of coffee.

Chapter Six

It hadn't worked.

He'd been busy for two days, he and Carly had done a dozen fun things and distracted themselves in a host of different ways, and the dread for Valentine's Day tomorrow and the wedding after that still filled his stomach like rocks.

Really? he thought to himself as they walked back into the inn lobby after their full day in Asheville. *You thought escaping to an entire town built on matrimonial bliss, and staying here over Valentine's Day to boot, was a good idea?* Sure, it wasn't home, where memories of Sandy loomed everywhere, but Matrimony Valley was proving to be a bad escape plan. Terrible, actually.

It's not the town's fault, he told himself. *You'd likely be miserable this week no mat-*

ter where you were. It was similar to what he'd told his boss when he'd asked to come back from bereavement leave a week early. *It hurts at home*, he'd told the man. *Might as well hurt here where I've got something useful to do.* The grief counselor told him to get Carly back into her usual routine—which meant part-time day care—and he certainly had no desire to wander the house in a lonesome fog.

Somehow the inn had sprouted even more Valentine's decorations today than yesterday. "Look at all the hearts, Daddy." On Sunday, Carly had pointed out the collection of knitted hearts that hung in the inn's front lobby windows. "They're like the one in Lulu's mom's shop. And I saw one when we had ice cream."

"Well, I just keep running into you two."

He turned to see Kelly holding a huge arrangement of red and white flowers with shiny foil hearts sticking out between the blooms and leaves. "That's…festive."

"It's so pretty," Carly said, reaching up to touch one of the sparkly hearts. "Are those the flowers we saw in your car today?"

"Some of them," Kelly replied. "They're for that big table over there." She tilted her head in the direction of the large round table sitting in the center of the lobby. "Lulu's at piano lessons, and I need someone to help me sprinkle the confetti that goes around it. Think I should ask your dad?"

Carly's love of all things glittery popped her eyes wide as she said, "Ask me! Ask me!"

"Carly! You could help me." She pasted a mock look of surprise on her face. "Why didn't I think of that?"

Bruce offered her a dubious look as the three of them walked over to the table with a big round silver platter at the center. He felt compelled to give her a hand when it became clear Kelly could barely maneuver the massive arrangement into place. The awkward size seemed to hinder more than the weight, which surprised him because the thing must have weighed twenty-five pounds. He kept assuming her small frame made her delicate, and she kept proving him wrong.

Carly fairly squealed when Kelly reached into her bag to produce a package of glittery pink, red and white hearts to scatter on the silver platter. She handed the package to Carly and said, "Would you like to do it all yourself?"

"Sure!" Carly exclaimed, immediately getting to work as Kelly and Bruce stepped back.

"She's a natural," Kelly remarked with a laugh. "She should do great as the flower girl on Saturday."

"We might have practiced a bit with some wood chips," Bruce admitted.

"Good for you, Dad." After a moment, she added, "So, do you dread this girliest of holidays? You don't strike me as the unicorns and glitter type, despite Carly's fascination."

He couldn't decide how to answer, given she was a florist and all. She probably loved all this stuff. "Truthfully?"

"Yes."

He looked around the living valentine of a town and rocked back on his heels. "I usually avoid it like the plague. Which makes me wonder why I thought hiding out in 'plague central' would be a good idea."

She stepped back a bit, gesturing him to join her out of Carly's hearing. "Seems to me you need an escape plan."

"A what?"

"An escape plan. Some days just need… avoiding for a while. Birthdays, special occasions, you know."

He stared, not expecting to hear that sort of thing from her.

"My late husband proposed on Valentine's Day, and it was two years before I could get through it without feeling like I was made of glass. Not exactly useful for someone in my profession. All the couples, all the well-meaning but ridiculous things people say to…well, people like you and me." She sighed. "Was your first Valentine's Day bad?" She shook her head. "Look at me, asking a dumb question like that. Of course it was."

"Torture," he said, watching Carly's joyful engrossment in arranging the confetti just right. "Or whatever word's worse than *torture*. Everybody was so carefully cheerful. Everybody tried to make sure I wasn't alone when being alone was the only thing I wanted. This year, I'd sort of hoped to avoid it altogether."

"Here?" She laughed. "Hide from Valentine's Day in Matrimony Valley? You're right—bad plan."

Bruce had heard the valley's transformation story at the hands of the present mayor. Maybe that's what had drawn him to have a longer stay in the town—it was a place that had fought its way back to life after an economic death nearly shut it down. The valley spoke to him that life's comebacks were still possible. It was an inspiring thought—on any day but today. "Like I said, I didn't quite think it through."

"No, sir," she countered. "You did not."

"Got any advice?" Asking a florist for advice on how to do an end run around Valentine's Day? Seriously?

"You know, the church throws a party for all the kids after school. I'm sure Lulu would love Carly to come. It might occupy a few hours."

He gave her a sideways glance. "Why did I know you'd suggest more church?"

She crossed her arms over her chest. "Fine. Just pick a few of your *101 Things to Do*, then."

She was teasing him. And he was enjoying it. That was scary. "You're going to this church thing?"

"Absolutely—wouldn't miss it."

"You sure you aren't swamped with deliveries or something?"

"Most are done by then. It's tonight that I'll be working until the wee hours." She lowered her voice. "Lulu and I actually do a sleepover at the shop, but don't let Carly know that or she may want to come along."

The church party seemed like the best option he had. He'd hoped to get Carly back outdoors, but that was looking unlikely. "I'm sure Carly would love to come to the church Valentine's Day party. But doesn't Lulu have other school friends her age she'd rather play with?"

He immediately regretted the remark as her face sank. "You'd think so, right? But Lulu has only one really good friend in town—

Jonah, the little son of Mayor Jean. Dads are invited, too, by the way. I'm sure Jonah's dad will be there, and you can meet him. But I'm sure you understand that little boys don't quite get into Valentine's Day the same way little girls do."

As if to underscore the fact, Carly danced around the table sprinkling confetti like a Cupidian fairy. Even if it made him slightly ill, all that girlie stuff made her happy. And sometimes, her capacity for simple happiness seemed like the only thing that kept him going. "We'd love to come." The "we" was a gross overstatement, but Bruce suspected she knew that.

"It won't be so awful, you know. There's good food, loads of other parents and the kids have a ball. And even if you end up thinking it is awful, you can always drown your sorrows in a mountain of baked goods and ice cream."

He frowned. "Not exactly my coping mechanism of choice. Guys don't really do the 'cry into a pint of ice cream' thing."

"Too bad. It's very effective. So what do 'guys' do to cope?" She raised an eyebrow, indicating she meant one particular guy—him.

How *did* he cope? It unnerved him that he didn't really have an answer for that. Because he mostly *didn't* cope. He just endured. All the grief had burned itself up inside him, leaving a hollow space that didn't seem to want to be filled with anything—certainly not with calories. In fact, he'd lost enough weight in the last two years that his doctor chided him at his last physical. His indulgence of Carly's sweet tooth recently was partially to see if anything really could be "delicious" anymore.

"Guys don't do anything."

Kelly planted one hand on her hip. "This, from a man in possession of all those shopping bags I saw this morning. It seems to me like retail therapy is your choice."

"That's different."

"No, I don't think it is."

When he glared at her, not in the least bit interested in being analyzed by someone who'd known him all of four days, she simply gathered her bag and offered an irritatingly knowing smile. "The party's in the church hall at 3:00 p.m. I'll tell Lulu you're both coming."

Wednesday afternoon, all but two of the deliveries had been made. The mountain of Valentine's Day arrangements had left her shop. She'd had a decent holiday—logistically and financially—and George had stayed up and running. Even so, all of Kelly's exhaustion evaporated at the sight of her friend when she walked into the church. "You're here!" she exclaimed as she gave Jean a big hug.

"Well, I thought I'd better show up in a few places, and Josh is here to handle most of the parental duties." Normally a bubbly personality, Jean today held tight to a glass of ginger ale and sank back onto her pair of chairs in the corner with her sprained ankle raised. "I'm really hoping to make the wedding, too."

"You will. It's going fine," Kelly said with confidence she didn't really feel. She'd been basking in Valentine's Day victory until an hour ago, when she reviewed her list of tasks for Tina and Darren's wedding and felt her heart sink at everything that still needed to be done—and the things, like the weather, that were out of her hands.

Jean smiled at her son and his father. "Look at Josh doing the dad thing like he's been at it all of Jonah's life." Josh was Jonah's biological father, but hadn't been in his life until a startling "God-incidence"—as Jean was known to call it—that brought him to Matrimony Valley with the town's first official wedding last May. The rekindling of Jean and Josh's love, and the blossoming relationship between father and son, was a truly happy story. After all, shouldn't the mayor of Matrimony Valley be a happily married woman?

"In a month he'll be better at sign language than I am," Jean went on. Her son had been profoundly deaf since birth, and much of the valley had learned the basics of sign language to help Jonah feel at home. Josh, who'd known no sign language before meeting his son, had applied his famous brilliance to the new skill with zeal, and Kelly watched him signing fast and happily with his son. "He's an amazing father. Really." The woman fairly glowed from love and happiness—and the new life growing within her.

Kelly squeezed her friend's hand. "And you're an amazing mother." She leaned in and whispered, "And soon you'll be twice as amazing."

"As soon as I can stop feeling twice as queasy," Jean whispered back.

"When are you going to tell everyone?"

"I want to get past the twelve-week mark, so maybe around Saint Patrick's Day." Jean gave Kelly a pleading look. "I've got to believe I'll feel better by then. I certainly don't want to stick you with any more weddings mostly on your own."

"Fortunately, this one is very low maintenance and comes with an advance team," Kelly replied, nodding toward Bruce, who was currently being a good sport and dipping a pair of frosting-doused cupcakes into bowls of sprinkles with his daughter.

"I'd think a maid of honor would be more help than a best man," Jean said as she sipped her ginger ale. "But the flower girl's adorable."

"Carly's so sweet. How that little girl goes so happily along with her father's frantic parenting is beyond me."

"Frantic?"

Kelly sat down beside her friend. "You know how Norm Myers just sort of froze solid when Polly died?" she said, citing one of the church's recent senior-citizen widowers. "Well, it seems some men go the other way. Bruce is in a high-speed orbit—my guess is that he does it to outrun the pain, bless him. I think he's just about to realize it doesn't work. I mean, I like to keep busy, but the guy makes me look like a tortoise."

"I don't think I realized his wife had died. You were nice to invite him here. Today can't be an easy day for him." Jean slipped her arm around Kelly. "Or you. Still."

"I'm better off than Mr. Frantic over there, that's for sure. I don't think five-year-olds should have quite such a packed schedule, especially on what's supposed to be a vacation. I've been encouraging Lulu to invite her places simply so the poor thing can catch her breath."

"Speaking of catching your breath, he is rather easy on the eyes, don't you think?"

Kelly furrowed her eyebrows. Bruce was a very handsome man, yes, but still an emotional minefield. "Stop that right now, Your Honor. Even if I were looking, which I'm not, I'd want less of a walking-wounded case—or in this case, I should say running wounded. Sprinting, actually."

"He does look a little lost, doesn't he?"

"A *little*?"

"Well, I still say you were nice to bring him here. And it's nice for us to have him here. Josh told me he was sure he'd be the only male of the species between ten and sixty."

Kelly looked around the room. Josh wasn't that far off. Aside from Bruce and Josh, the party consisted of kids, moms and a smattering of grandparents. Bruce and Josh really were the only men present even close to their age. So when Lulu introduced Carly to Jonah, carefully spelling out Carly's name in sign language before the trio of children began eating their cupcakes together, it wasn't at all surprising that Josh brought Bruce over to join Kelly and Jean's conversation.

"Finally, someone to talk basketball with

over cupcakes who won't show me pictures of his grandchildren," Josh said with a laugh.

"Poor Josh," Jean offered, chuckling herself. "He doesn't get out for cupcakes with the guys nearly as often as he should."

Bruce tried to play along. "It's a sad day when a man can't enjoy a good cupcake with his buddies." His words were teasing, but his tone was tight and strained.

That set Josh laughing. "Where'd you find this guy?"

"The elk wedding," Jean replied. "Bruce is best man."

"I decided to take some time off and come in early," Bruce said as he tried to figure out which angle was best for attacking the huge mound of frosting and sprinkles. Instead, he gave up and set it on the table next to him, stuffing his hands rigidly into his pockets.

"I did that for my stepsister's wedding. And after that first visit, I couldn't stay away." Josh took a bite of his own confection.

For so long, as the local economy spiraled deeper into decline, all people could think about was how to leave this valley. Now, thanks to Mayor Jean and the Matrimony Valley campaign, people came. And stayed. Someone like Bruce looked as if he needed a place like Matrimony Valley to slow him down and bring him back into life instead of running around on the outside edges of life.

"I've got no interest in relocating," Bruce offered as Josh licked a glob of frosting off one finger. "Oh, don't get me wrong, it's a nice break. Being here, I mean. But this town is a tad small for my taste. And six hours from work. Makes for a bit of a commute, even if they let me take the helicopter to get home— which they don't." His words came out in the short burst of a man trying too hard to look like he was having fun. Maybe it hadn't been the best idea to invite him.

"Hey, I came from California," Josh said. "You gotta be careful—this valley has a way of growing on you." With that, Josh gave his wife a gentle kiss. "Want half of my cupcake, Your Honor?"

"No thanks." Jean looked at the cupcake as if the sight alone sent her stomach tumbling. Very deliberately, she directed her gaze to Bruce. "Matrimony Valley is a lovely place to live. My family has been here for four generations."

"That's nice," Bruce said. He looked so uneasy. *Stop worrying about it*, Kelly told herself. *We host weddings. It's not our place to repair families.* Still, as she gazed at Jonah, Lulu and Carly happily running and playing with each other, she couldn't help but think that the valley she'd called home for all her life had indeed repaired her family when death broke it apart. And it had repaired Jean's, as well. As for the fidgeting man in front of her, however, it was hard to believe restoration could ever come to someone like Bruce.

"I'll go tell Lulu I'll be back to pick her up at five when the party's over. I've got two more deliveries today, and then I need to get everything in order for Darren and Tina. Plus, Samantha Douglas arrives tomorrow." Kelly looked at Josh. "Maybe try to see if you can get those three to eat something other than just frosting?"

Josh responded by swallowing half the frosting on his own cupcake. "Not a chance."

"He's impossible," Jean bemoaned.

"Hey, you wouldn't want me any other way," Josh teased, taking his wife's hand.

Holding hands. It had been one of her favorite things about being with Mark. Lulu held her hand all the time, but it wasn't the same. *Now I'm getting sentimental? Keep me busy, Lord.*

Staying busy to outrun the grief. Wasn't that exactly the thing she'd judged Bruce for doing? *You're being awfully hard on a guy who is just doing his best to cope.*

"Can I walk out with you for a minute?" Bruce asked, surprising her. "I've got a question about the…boutin-whatevers for the wedding," he said. "Josh said he'd watch Carly, and she looks like she's having a ball so…"

Bruce had looked okay—or close to okay—at first, but now his eyes held the familiar "get me out of here" panic she remembered from some parties and events in the months after Mark died. Granted, she didn't need further distraction after a busy day like today, but Bruce clearly needed an excuse to leave despite the fun Carly was having. Certain situations just had a way of making a soul feel excruciatingly single, and despite her good intentions, she'd plunked him down in the middle of one. The least she could do was give him an escape route. That was, after all, why she'd suggested the party in the first place.

"Boutonnieres," she corrected, then shrugged. "Sure. Actually, I can use someone of your height to give me a hand with something over at the shop, if that'd be okay with you and Josh will watch the kids."

"Glad to help," he said, relief filling his features. "Whatever you need."

I think this is more about what you need,

she thought as she grabbed her coat and let Carly and Lulu know they'd come back at the end of the party.

Chapter Seven

Bruce followed Kelly into the shop. "Um… thanks. For giving me an out back there, I mean. I thought it'd be okay…but it wasn't."

"I should have just offered to pick Carly up and bring her along with Lulu and myself," Kelly replied as she switched on the shop lights. "I don't know why I thought you might have a good time."

"Well, Carly's definitely having a good time," he said, looking out the window back toward the church. "That's what matters. I'm glad for that, really I am."

"That's good," she said. He turned back to see her pulling things out of the glass cooling cabinets that made up the back wall of the storefront. The light in the largest one blinked a bit, and it made a troublesome noise. She set a vase down on the counter and looked at him.

"You don't really have any questions about the boutonnieres, do you?"

"Only why we have to wear them. But other than that, no."

She turned back to the cooler and began pulling out a second vase. "You can't outrun it, you know." The weary resignation in her tone dug under his ribs in what Sandy might have called one of her "sharp truths." He'd not really noticed before now how exhaustion pulled down Kelly's shoulders.

"What?" he said, despite knowing exactly what she was talking about.

"Slowing down won't make it hurt more, you know. And staying on the go all the time will just wear you down. I learned that the hard way, ending up with pneumonia my first winter without Mark." She began wrapping some crackly clear paper around one of the smaller arrangements. "Why'd you come here, Bruce?"

"For Tina and Darren's wedding."

"No, that's why you'd come Thursday. Why'd you come so many days early?"

"I told you already. To spend some time away with Carly."

Kelly unwound a long string of red ribbon from a collection of spools hung on a rod. "And you can't spend time with Carly in Kinston?"

Maybe he would have been better off sticking with the party. "Did anyone ever tell you how pushy and nosy you are?"

She clipped the ribbon off with a firm *snip*. "Lots. I've got no plans to stop, either."

Clearly she wasn't going to let the question drop, so he might as well answer it. Even though she should know the answer already. "Kicking around the house... I hate it, okay? Didn't you feel like that? Like there's too much pain lurking in the corners?"

She got a funny look on her face. "No. I love the memories in our house. I couldn't live anywhere else, I don't think. Don't forget, Bruce, that you got a chance to say your goodbyes. Some of us weren't so fortunate. We've got to hang on to whatever's left, even if it's lurking in the corners."

"Fortunate?" he shot back. "It didn't feel fortunate to watch my wife die. To watch her disappear under a pile of chemicals and side effects and treatments. To have Carly's last images of her mother be a sickly shadow of the person I married. So no, I don't feel fortunate. I feel cheated. Robbed. Sandy was the healthiest person I knew, so will someone explain to me why God chose to reward that with cancer? Why Carly has to know that mommies can die? Can you and your pretty little church explain that to me?"

Kelly went completely still, the red ribbon dangling from her hands. She stared silently at him, hurt narrowing her eyes.

Bruce felt like a total, uncontrollable jerk, overtaken by some strange force bent on unleashing the storm of feelings that had been hiding behind the fog. She didn't deserve what he'd just done to her, not at all.

"Wow," he said quietly, wiping his hands down his face. "That was… I don't have an excuse for that."

She didn't reply. The shop was completely silent save for the stuttered, struggling humming of the cooler behind her.

"You invited Carly and me to a party and then got me out of there when it…" He turned and looked out the window, unable to meet her pained eyes. How was he ever going to make it through the wedding at this rate? "It's like I'm some kind of grief bomb this week, and as nice as everyone has been, your whole town is just a collection of people holding matches ready to light the fuse."

There was a long, raw pause before her voice came from behind him. "No one's doing this to you, Bruce. You are doing it to yourself."

I am not! he wanted to shout back, but

instead he just stared out the window and fumed. After a glowering moment, he noticed that a handful of white flakes fluttered across the light spilling out onto the street from the shop window. "Well, here it comes."

"Here what comes?" she snapped in reply. "Another lecture from me? No, I'm done helping or advising or meddling. You don't have to worry about me poking my nose into your life anymore except for the wedding."

He deserved every bit of the sharpness her words held. She'd had good intentions and he'd been a total grump.

"No," he said, turning around to face her. "Here comes the snow. Look."

By the time Kelly gathered Lulu from the party, the small fluffy flakes had turned to great big heavy ones. Tina would get her four perfect inches, and likely more. The weather report hinted that the coming snow would pack more of a punch than just "pretty frosting," as Lulu put it.

What's worse, the snow hadn't waited until tomorrow afternoon, after Samantha arrived. A storm could impede the writer's arrival into Matrimony Valley. And then there was the bride and groom and the whole wedding party, with the exception of the aggravating best man and adorable flower girl. Who knew what the weather would be like on the days those guests were coming in?

Lulu looked up from the book she was reading. "All this snow means Carly will get to go sledding now, right? I told her when we left the party that she and her dad could use our sleds if the inn doesn't have some."

Kelly was thankful Lulu hadn't noticed the chill now looming between her and Bruce. Lulu just wanted her new friend to have fun. Kelly loved her daughter's natural generosity. It had been one of the things that first attracted her to Mark, and it pleased her so to see it live on in their daughter. Mark had always lived in a world where there always seemed to be more than enough of everything.

Except time. If he'd have had more time, who knows what amazing things he could have done. Or even small, simple things, like taking his daughter and her new friend sledding.

Lulu put down her book and came up to the window. "It's starting to snow harder. Wouldn't it be great if they canceled school?"

Kelly gave Lulu a squeeze. "You wish. You'd love to get out of that spelling test, wouldn't you?" Lulu may have inherited Mark's generosity, but she also inherited Kelly's lack of spelling prowess. It was years before Kelly could correctly spell many flower names—she might have been better suited to working with all of Marvin's simple ice-cream flavors.

"Who wants to spell *believe* when you could be busy sledding?"

Kelly laughed. "Good point."

"And you know what I wish?"

"What's that, sweetheart?"

"I wish we'd get snowed in. I'd love it if we got so much snow that Carly and her dad had to stay a whole extra week after the wedding."

Those girls really had connected strongly. "Our bride and groom might have a word to say about that wish. What about all of them and their wedding guests?"

"Oh, well, they can stay, too." Lulu got a dreamy look on her face. "But don't you think Carly and her dad are extra nice?"

"They're very nice. I'm glad you've been such a friend to her. Now go get just as friendly with those spelling words while I take these clean towels upstairs."

"Sure," Lulu agreed—a little too easily. "You go on upstairs and I'll wait right here."

Something's up, Kelly thought as she gathered the towels from the dryer and piled them into the laundry basket to head upstairs. By the time she reached the linen closet in the upstairs bathroom, however, she didn't need to wonder any further. Taped to her bathroom mirror was an elaborately decorated valentine.

What a sweetheart. It was just like Lulu to make sure she felt cared for on such a busy day. "Have a happy heart today," the card proclaimed with a cheerful, smiley-faced heart full of glitter.

Kelly opened the card to read the signature. "Love, Bruce." In a child's handwriting.

Oh, dear.

Kelly walked to her bedroom phone and dialed Jean.

"Hey there." Jean sounded tired. "Everything okay?"

"That depends," Kelly replied. "All my deliveries are done, and except for all this snow, things are fine so far with the wedding." She sighed and sat down in the rocking chair beside her bedroom window. "No, my problems are of another sort."

"What's up?"

"I just got a lovely valentine."

"Oh, well, that sounds nice. Jonah gave me one, too. They must have made some at the party."

"Mine didn't come from Lulu. Or at least I'm not supposed to think it did."

"You want to explain that?" Jean asked.

"I'm supposed to *think* mine came from Bruce Lohan."

There was a pause before Jean replied, "Oh. *Oh*, I can see what you mean."

Kelly looked at the red card with its dousing of happy glitter and message inside. "I think Lulu and Carly have gotten a few ideas into their heads. What am I supposed to do about this?"

"Well, now, that depends. How would you have felt if the card really did come from Bruce?"

"Considering we just had an argument over at the shop this afternoon, I'm not so sure. No matter what, the girls should not be matching us up."

"Have you talked to Lulu about this?"

Suddenly today felt like it had lasted a week. Kelly looked out the window at the steadily falling snow. "I wimped out and called you first. Lulu's never even mentioned wanting someone else in my life until now, much less pulled a stunt like this. It's hard to know what Carly and she are thinking." She gulped. "Actually, it's *not* hard to know what they're thinking, is it?" She sunk back in the chair, suddenly realizing something. "Oh, no. Do you think Carly made one just like it for

Bruce?" The thought of Bruce finding something pink and sparkly on his hotel bathroom mirror with her "signature" on it made her face flush. What would he think of such a stunt? He'd know the card wasn't really from her, wouldn't he? Still, how would she face that man in the morning?

"Carly's too young to write, isn't she?" Jean asked.

"Maybe, but Lulu's not." She could just imagine the two girls, giggling and conspiring as they crafted the forged valentines. "Lulu made all these comments tonight about wishing we'd get a big snowstorm that would force Carly and her dad to stay. I thought it was just about her wanting to spend more time with Carly. Now I feel like those words have taken on a whole new layer of meaning." Of course she felt a speck of attraction for the man—he was handsome and cared a great deal about his daughter. But he was a pilot and, quite frankly, a mess. It was lovely that their daughters found such a friendship with each other, but it should not go any further than that.

"Matrimony Valley's littlest matchmakers," Jean said with a laugh. "I know you're upset, but it's kind of adorable, when you think about it."

"Not from where I sit. I need to talk to Lulu.

Tonight. Don't I? Nip this little scheme in the bud right now?"

"That's up to you."

"Say a prayer for wisdom for this tired mom, will you? I'm going downstairs to tell my daughter to leave the matchmaking to the grown-ups."

Jean laughed again. "So that means that I, as a grown-up, can play matchmaker to the valley florist?"

"No. I'm tired, I barely made it through Valentine's Day and I've got a hugely important wedding in three days. No matchmaking. Not with Bruce Lohan or anybody. The only man I want in my life is the refrigerator repairman or any man giving away free florist vans. Or Mr. Coffee."

"Okay, then. Call me tomorrow and let me know how that conversation went. I'm going to have my valentine bring me another ginger ale and then I'm going to bed."

Carly slipped into bed with a wide, happy smile plastered all over her face. "I had gobs and gobs of fun today, Daddy." She remembered Sandy's favorite term for a wonderful day. That pleased him endlessly, and he kissed Carly's forehead with bittersweet tenderness.

"I'm glad."

"Did you have a fun day, too?"

Hmm. How to answer that? It had certainly not been a "gobs and gobs of fun" day. Would Carly understand that this Valentine's Day never had a chance of being good for him? "It wasn't horrible," didn't seem a fair response, so he went with a half-truth: "I had a fun day with you. Good night, valentine." He turned off all the lights except the unicorn night-light they'd brought from home and shut the adjoining door partway.

Walking into his room, he tried to unpack the crazy day. The description he'd growled at Kelly was accurate. He did feel like an emotional bomb amid a sea of lit matches. And *boom!*—he'd exploded right in front of her. The last person who deserved it, even if she was the first person who might understand. Honestly, he felt as if she'd come at him with an imaginary set of shears, determined to hack away at the nest of thorns he'd carefully built around himself.

And wouldn't she love that image. That woman got under his skin. Her constant poking into his life made him crazy, but her declaration of being done with it bugged him far more. Couldn't she just leave him alone without declaring him a hopeless case?

Then again, had he given her any reason

not to throw up her hands in defeat? He'd said those mean things to her, practically goading her into giving up on him. *No more help or advising or meddling*, she'd declared, and he couldn't blame her.

Then again, she'd said some pretty nosy, gutsy things to him. He took the risk and told her what he was feeling—not particularly well or eloquently, granted—and she'd basically told him it was all his fault. That he was making himself miserable.

What human being would choose to make himself feel like this? Willingly hoard all this anger and sorrow and pain? She, of all people, should understand how much he wanted to come back to life, to stop feeling this horrible mix of empty and shredded.

He liked her advice almost as much as he hated it. Her irritating meddling never felt like coddling. Annoying as her scrutiny was, Kelly was the first person in far too long who actually saw *him*, not just the man who lost Sandy, or the single dad who was out of his depth. And while he wished that viewpoint didn't somehow give her a license to give him a few sharp kicks, part of him knew one came with the other.

Bruce lay down on the bedspread, falling back with his hands behind his head. He stared up at the ceiling until he realized something crinkled underneath his hands. Rolling over, he pulled the bedspread down to reveal a handmade valentine card tucked on top of the pillow. "Be Mine," it said in bright pink letters scrawled across the white paper, a cloud of tiny red hearts fluttering all around the words. How sweet of Lulu to help Carly make him a valentine. Their friendship would be Carly's favorite part of this vacation, he had no doubt of that.

Smiling, Bruce sat up and opened the card. "Love, Kelly" was not at all what he expected to see. And here he'd just figured Carly's silly smile was an expression of pure happiness, not glee at having played Matrimony Valley Matchmaker. This was trouble.

He fell back onto the bed with a groan as he realized what must be true: somewhere in her house Kelly Nelson was likely in possession of a similarly forged valentine. With his name inside.

Of course they both knew the cards were the girls' doing. And naturally, this presented an unbelievably sticky problem. One that had to be set right, and as quickly as possible. But the thought of Kelly somewhere beyond all that falling snow, looking at her card with the same wiggly, inexplicable, "caught with your hand in the cookie jar" feeling made him want to jump out of his skin. Most of him knew the girls were simply acting on a wish to be together, pairing him up with Kelly for the sake of their own friendship rather than from any belief that he and Kelly were actually in love.

A small, highly irritating part of him latched onto the absurd notion that the girls had picked up on some irrational current of attraction between himself and that nosy, controlling florist.

But that was impossible. Because it wasn't there. It couldn't, shouldn't be there.

He'd very, very carefully bottled up any possibility of there being something between them. What right did his own flesh and blood have to go yanking out the stopper?

Now what? Bruce was at such a loss for the next appropriate step that he hopped off the bed to pace the room. Out the hotel window, he could see the darkened windows of Love in Bloom through the curtain of falling snow. He had only the shop number from their wedding tasks, and she clearly wasn't there. He didn't have her home phone or cell numbers, and he certainly wasn't going to call downstairs or contact anyone in Matrimony Valley to get it. Besides, what on earth would he say? He could walk there, but he couldn't leave Carly. Besides, he wasn't at all prepared to discuss this face-to-face. And he couldn't explain the nonsense of this to Carly, because she was asleep.

He stared into Carly's bedroom, where she slept soundly after such a fun day. How could he possibly sleep now?

He'd said things to Kelly Nelson that he'd not said to anyone. The lure of her mutual experience, the understanding he saw in her eyes, had untangled some of his knots, and that scared him. She had all his wounds, had lost someone without even the bittersweet goodbye he'd been given with Sandy, and she was making it work. She seemed happy. Lulu seemed to be doing fine. It was as if seeing that slightest glimpse of real survival made his barely hanging-on version of it feel grimmer than it already did.

The most unwelcome memory came back to him, making it all worse. It had been one of those nights when Sandy's pain kept them both awake far into the small and scary hours. *I pray for her*, she'd said. She'd been holding his hand, and he'd been making circles on the back of it the way he did to distract her from the pain. Her voice had become so thin she barely sounded like Sandy.

Carly? he'd asked, choking back tears. They both knew there weren't too many days left.

Her, too. Sandy had managed to smile. *But for who's next.*

Her hysterectomy already decreed they'd have no more natural children, even if they had time. *Next?*

The next woman who gets to have your heart.

It was the one time he'd allowed himself to cry in front of her. *There's only you*, he'd sobbed into her bony chest, hating how her ribs pressed against his cheek. *There will only be you.*

I hope not, she'd said, stroking his hair. *I envy her. You'll be such a silver fox when you're old.* He remembered hating how her laughter dissolved so quickly into rasping coughs.

He felt old now. Much older than he was, that's for sure. Too old to face a long, sleepless night stewing in the fact that his daughter hoped his next valentine should be Kelly Nelson.

Chapter Eight

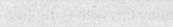

He was hiding.

To the average person, it would look like a man had simply decided to take his daughter out for a walk in the gorgeous snow-frosted morning down the street to Bliss Bakery for hot cocoa and doughnuts. But Bruce knew better. He was trying to stay out of sight of Kelly and Lulu until he could talk this out with Carly, and for some reason staying at the inn made it feel like she could appear at any minute.

Of course, she had a talent for running into him wherever he was, which meant she could show up here, as well. Still, hiding here meant at least she wouldn't find him if she came looking for him at the inn.

And knowing her, she would. Kelly had to be as unsettled by the appearance of these valentines as he was. It had been a terrible night. He couldn't stop himself from wondering what she was thinking about, how she'd reacted, whether or not she was lying awake thinking about what he was thinking about… The whole thing was just one huge ball of sleepless anxiety.

Finally, in the wee hours of the morning, Bruce decided how he wanted to deal with it. And it meant settling this with Carly first before facing Kelly and Lulu, which would come soon enough.

"Carly, hon," he began as they settled in with an indulgent mug of cocoa for her and the strongest coffee the bakery had for him. Along with, of course, doughnuts covered in red, pink and white sprinkles. "I want to talk to you about the valentine I found on my pillow last night."

She gave him a wide-eyed, innocent-looking blink. "What valentine? Did you get one?"

He pushed out a breath and leaned in toward her. "You and Lulu made that valentine, didn't you?"

Though her eyes stayed wide, the innocent look left her face. She fidgeted, but said nothing.

"Please don't lie to me, Carly. Not ever, and especially not about this."

When she still didn't confess, he gave her his most serious look and said, "Carly Anne Lohan…"

"Maybe," she said very quietly.

"Why?" he asked, even though it wasn't hard to guess the answer.

Carly poked at the frosting on her doughnut. "I like her."

"Lulu is a very nice friend, I know."

"But I like her mom, too. She's nice. You smile at her when you think I'm not looking."

Bruce couldn't remember smiling at Kelly—at least he'd tried not to—but he also couldn't argue that she did, for reasons that made very little sense, seem to loosen something tightly bound in him. "Miss Kelly is a nice person, I agree," he admitted. "But what you and Lulu did was wrong. It wasn't the truth."

Carly's bottom lip stuck out in a guilty pout. "We were wishing. I was wishing Miss Kelly and Lulu were in our family, and Lulu was wishing you and me were in her family. You like her, and Lulu says she likes you. We were just helping, weren't we?"

Bruce pinched the bridge of his nose. He had to step very carefully here. "Did you hear me say I liked Miss Kelly? In a valentine kind of way? Did you hear me say those words?"

"Not really," Carly admitted, looking down for a moment before she added, "But you don't go away around her. And she's soooo nice. And pretty. I like her and Lulu a lot, Dad."

"I know you do. And I suppose she is…kind of…pretty. But that doesn't…." How was he going to make her understand? "Sweetheart, grown-ups have to decide things like this for ourselves. This isn't something you and Lulu get to decide for Miss Kelly and me, no matter how much you might wish for it." He felt like he had to ask. "Do you wish for another mom?"

Her eyes just about broke his heart when she said, "Sometimes."

"That's okay," he said, taking her small hand. "Every little girl wants a mommy, and it doesn't—" he had to swallow hard on account of the huge lump that rose in his throat "—it doesn't mean we love Mom in heaven any less."

"Okay." That little bottom lip quivered, threatening to undo him. He had expected this conversation to be awkward and difficult. He hadn't expected it to slice through him this way. Suddenly, his inability to heal seemed like it was harming her, denying her something every little girl needed.

"Now, if the time ever comes that I think

there's a new mommy to come into our family, I promise you we'll talk about it. A lot." The idea was distant and impossible, wasn't it? It certainly felt frightening.

"Couldn't it be Miss Kelly?"

Bruce didn't have a good answer to so direct a question. If he forced himself to really consider it, he'd have to admit it was possible. Under different circumstances, maybe months from now, Kelly Nelson could be someone he might consider dating. She was, in fact, the first woman who even remotely struck him as someone he might want in his life. If he was ready to date. Which he absolutely wasn't. "This isn't the time." He knew that wouldn't be enough of an answer for Carly.

It wasn't. "Why not?" she persisted.

The best defense he could come up with was deflection. "Well, for one thing, this weekend is supposed to be about Miss Tina and Mr. Darren getting married."

"I know. But you do like Miss Kelly, don't you?"

He liked her, sort of. She was pushy and a bit of a control freak, but she was also creative and smart and brave. He certainly liked the amazing way she had with Carly. "That's not the point."

"Why?"

Five-year-olds and their "why?" questions. "Because the point is you put Miss Kelly's name on a card that she didn't write. And did you make one for Miss Kelly with my name on it? Without my permission? Saying things I didn't give you permission to say?"

There was a long, sniffly pause before Carly said, "S'pose."

"Not 'suppose,' you did. And while I understand why you did it, it's still wrong. And while Miss Kelly gets to decide what Lulu has to do about it, I get to decide what you have to do." He sat up straight. "And my decision is that you owe Miss Kelly an apology."

That brought a stricken look to Carly's eyes. "Really?"

He'd decided this was the best way to deal with the valentines. To address the issue of their deception rather than the stickier concept that the girls had picked up on an attraction between Kelly and himself. "Yes, really." He pointed across the street. "We can see the flower shop windows from here. And when Miss Kelly opens up and the lights go on over there, you and I are going to walk across the street and you're going to apologize to her for putting her name on that valentine without her permission."

Carly's eyes glistened as her bottom lip stuck out farther. "Do I hafta?"

She was so adorable that it was hard not to smile at her, but he needed to stay serious. Sweet as the intention was, it was still deception, and this matchmaking scheme had to be squelched immediately. "Yes, you 'hafta.'"

She looked at her doughnut. "I'm gonna need this whole doughnut. Maybe two."

Now that was 100 percent Sandy. The day she'd made a whopping mistake at her work and had to fess up to her boss, she'd eaten half a chocolate cake. "Two doughnuts is okay, but even three wouldn't change what you have to do."

"Can I have the one with chocolate sprinkles next?"

He hid the smile from his face until he walked up to the counter and pointed out the chocolate sprinkle doughnut to the brown-haired woman behind the counter with "Yvonne" stitched into her blue apron.

"I'm sorry," Yvonne said as she lifted the doughnut out of the case with a square of waxed paper. "I wasn't meaning to eavesdrop, but I gotta say, that was some pretty impressive parenting."

The pleasant sense of affirmation warred with embarrassment. The only thing that would make this whole situation worse was anyone else knowing about it. "Um, thanks."

"Carly has gumption, that's for sure."

At least that he could agree with. "It was just a bit of a misunderstanding, I'm afraid." Understatement of the year.

The bakery owner gave him an all-too-knowing look. "But Kelly's a pretty amazing woman, too. Not that it's any of my business—"

"It's not," he cut her off, not liking how everyone in this town seemed totally comfortable sticking their noses in everyone else's business. The inn offered room service—why hadn't he dealt with so delicate a matter in the privacy of his room?

"I'm just saying," she said with a wide smile as if he hadn't just tried to end the conversation. "Having a thing for Kelly Nelson isn't the worst thing a guy like yourself could do."

Bruce considered marching out to the "Welcome to Matrimony Valley" sign and adding a panel that read "Beware of Meddling." He scowled at the baker. "I'll just leave the advice and take the doughnut, if you don't mind."

"On the house," she said, sliding the doughnut across the counter to him. "Both."

Kelly leaned up against her refrigerator. "She's here?" she said into the phone as Hailey called to let her know Samantha Douglas had just checked in. "Already? I thought she was coming at eleven?"

"They wanted to get ahead of the weather. She and her photographer walked in about fifteen minutes ago. The photographer guy just dumped his bags at the desk and went right back outside to photograph, gushing about the beauty of new-fallen snow."

"Oh, well, that sounds promising. It is pretty out there."

"Samantha didn't seem to share his delight. I gave her our best room outside of the bridal suite, and she still frowned. And older than I was expecting. She's really the one who writes the reviews for wedding venues? You've got your work cut out for you—she's one picky lady."

Kelly had to admit to the same reaction on her many phone calls to the writer. "She does seem picky. But lots of people read her. And even more follow her online."

"Well, I hope the photographer gets a bunch of great shots. The inn looks terrific dusted with snow. The whole avenue does."

"I'm glad I delivered those gift bags to you while I was there yesterday," Kelly said as she dumped more grounds into the coffee maker. "Picky or not, we need to impress her." This wasn't the day for Samantha Douglas to show up early. Lulu was barely awake, and Kelly was yawning herself. She'd lain awake for hours after a long conversation with Lulu about what she and Carly had done. While she'd managed to get through to Lulu that how they'd gone about it was wrong, Lulu just couldn't see why the grown-ups didn't understand how perfect a solution the match was.

You like him, Mom, Lulu had offered, as if that solved it all. *And he likes you. And Carly and I are super-good friends already. It's perfect.*

That's not how things like this happen, hadn't convinced Lulu in the slightest. She'd finally sent Lulu to bed with the promise that she would write an apology note to Bruce in the morning. For the next hour—and several times after that—Kelly talked herself out of dialing the inn and asking for Bruce's room. She didn't know what she'd say if she could reach him anyway. When the snow had delayed the start of school, Kelly was grateful for the chance at a slow morning. Now, with Samantha already here, who knew when they would find time to deal with the girls' misguided scheme?

"Look, I know Samantha Douglas can do a

lot for us," Hailey was saying on the other end of the line, bringing Kelly's thoughts back to the present. "She'll get top-notch treatment, don't you worry. But she does seem rather worried about a heavier storm coming in."

Get in line, thought Kelly, squinting out at the white landscape. The bride and groom were both due in tonight. "Where is she now?"

"The photographer just came back in. I'll go seat them for breakfast."

Kelly hit the brew button on the coffee machine. "I'll be there in twenty minutes." Bruce, Carly and the whole valentine tangle would just have to wait until Samantha Douglas was settled.

"Okay. See you then."

Kelly put her hands over her eyes and forced in a deep breath. *Stay close, Lord. It's gonna be a crazy hard day.* "Change of plans, young lady," Kelly said to Lulu, who was pulling a box of cereal out of the cabinet. "We're going to meet the *Southeast Nuptials* reporter at the inn and have breakfast there. I'll walk you to the bus stop after that, and you can write your letter to Mr. Lohan tonight."

"Waffles!" Lulu exclaimed, as if nothing at all had gone amiss. "And I'll get to see Carly!" she said as she took off up the stairs.

And that. Going to the inn could mean running into Bruce without time to really talk, and that would certainly be awkward, but there was no help for it. He had to be feeling as odd about last night's turn of events as she was, and they'd just have to deal with it when the opportunity came.

Fortunately, there was no sign of either Bruce or Carly as she and Lulu sat down at a table near Samantha Douglas and her photographer a short time later.

"Have you enjoyed the inn's famous waffles?" Kelly asked, noticing the remnants of the inn's signature heart-shaped waffles on the woman's plate.

"They're delicious," Lulu chimed in.

"Very charming," Samantha replied, in a voice that didn't sound charmed at all.

"I'm glad you came up early. The town is so beautiful in a coat of new snow, don't you think?"

"I got some great shots," offered the photographer.

"Aren't you worried about travel issues?" Samantha asked. "I wouldn't want to get stuck up here on account of ice or snow."

"We can handle weather," Kelly declared. "Besides, I like to think we do winter weddings with the same creativity as our summer ones. This one really shows off what Matrimony Valley can do, Ms. Douglas."

Samantha sipped her coffee. "So you keep saying."

"I'll personally guarantee your safe travel no matter what the weather. Even if I have to drive you in my own van myself."

"Of course you'll comp our rooms should we end up stranded?" Samantha adjusted her glasses, looking as if being stranded in Matrimony Valley presented a highly unpleasant prospect.

"Absolutely," Kelly reiterated. "Your interview with the bakery isn't for several hours. Would you like to start with a tour through town?"

"I suppose." She reached into her posh handbag and began flipping through the screen on her phone. "Don, are they still saying the worst of the storm will stay north of here?"

"Lulu!" Carly came running through the dining room doors, having spotted her new friend. She froze when her eyes met Kelly's. Lulu clearly wasn't the only one who received "a talking-to" after last night.

"Carly, stop…" Bruce came in behind her, his own face contorting with discomfort upon seeing Kelly. The whole moment was excruciating enough without Samantha Douglas watching. "We were waiting for you to open up the shop."

"Oh, well, I'm here, with Samantha Douglas from *Southeastern Nuptials Magazine.*"

Upon a nudge from Bruce, Carly mumbled, "Hello, Miss Kelly."

"Good morning, Mr. Bruce," Lulu mumbled with an equally sheepish tone.

No one else said anything for a long moment while everyone avoided everyone else's eyes. When Kelly could bear it no longer, she said, "Samantha, this is the wedding's best man, Bruce Lohan. He came in early to make a vacation of visiting Matrimony Valley with his daughter."

He coughed at first, but found his voice and extended a hand to shake Samantha's. "Charming little town, isn't it?"

"I love it here," added Carly.

"It's certainly rustic." When Kelly couldn't quite say if Ms. Douglas considered that a positive trait, she confirmed her opinion by adding, "If you like this sort of thing."

"I think it's pretty," Carly proclaimed. "And it has reindeer."

"Elk," Bruce corrected, although Kelly didn't think Samantha Douglas held either in much esteem. "My daughter, Carly, is the flower girl for the wedding. And Kelly's correct—we chose to spend a week's vacation here on top of the event to enjoy everything the town has to offer."

"Well, it certainly is out of the way." The writer's declaration fell rather short of a compliment.

"We prefer to think of it as secluded," Kelly amended. "Accessible to bigger cities, but peaceful. With exciting, memorable weddings."

"No one can say you aren't determined."

That was one way to put it. "We all are." Figuring the moment couldn't get worse, Kelly decided to risk a question. "Bruce, do you think Darren and Tina would consent to give an interview?" Not that it wasn't a dicey proposition to let the press have access to the bride. Brides could get crazy right before a wedding, even one as laid-back as Tina seemed. But Samantha looked like she'd need a lot of convincing that this was going to be a great wedding. Someone had to get her to see that "rustic" was a good thing, not the flaw Ms. Douglas seemed to view it as.

"I don't see why you can't ask," he replied.

That was good enough. "Great." She turned to Samantha. "Should I see if I can arrange a coffee this afternoon when they arrive?"

"Yes. Can you take me over to the shop to see your designs now?"

She hadn't gotten Lulu's breakfast. She hadn't gotten her own. School was in an hour. She'd come nowhere near addressing the girls' antics last night. But Kelly smiled and said, "Of course." She checked her watch, scrambling for how to make this work. "Just…give me a minute to get Lulu settled for breakfast and school."

"Why don't you let me help you with that?" Bruce stepped in. "I've got something I've been meaning to discuss with the girls." He leveled a serious look at both of them, sending Carly sinking into the chair Kelly would have occupied. "And then Carly and I can walk Lulu to the bus stop for school."

If she didn't have the time to deal with this right now herself, Bruce was the next best thing. They'd have to talk about it between themselves—and soon—but the priority was to straighten out the girls, and Bruce seemed ready to take that on.

"Thanks, Bruce," she said. "That'd be a great help." Kelly looked squarely at Lulu. "You will listen carefully to everything Mr. Bruce tells you, won't you?"

"Yes, ma'am," Lulu replied.

Not the solution I planned, Kelly thought as

she gathered her things to take Samantha over to the shop, *but today seems to be the day for plans going out the window.*

Chapter Nine

Despite multiple efforts, everything seemed to get in the way of Kelly's talking to Bruce about what had happened. Samantha required a lot of attention, snow complicated all sorts of things and then Bruce was called upon to go fetch Darren when his truck broke down on the way into town. What else could go wrong?

"You finally made it!" Kelly exclaimed as a rather bedraggled-looking Bruce, Darren and another groomsman stomped the snow off their boots in the Hailey's Inn Love lobby well after two.

"We did," announced Carly, who looked rather bedraggled, as well. The round trip to fetch Darren shouldn't have taken more than an hour, but had required three thanks to the weather. Already they were talking about canceling Lulu's school tomorrow. The bride's flight from where she was visiting with her parents in Ohio had been delayed—twice—and forecasts now called for a worrisome see-saw between melt and freeze over the next twenty-four hours.

"How's Tina?" Kelly was almost afraid to ask.

"Frazzled. I keep telling her not to worry, that we've still got plenty of time, even if she doesn't make it in until tomorrow." Darren looked around to his companions and shrugged. "Well, she did say she wanted snow."

"And snow you got," Kelly replied cheerfully. "It's going to be a beautiful wedding, Darren. Every wedding has one snag, and look at you—you've gotten it out of the way already."

"I suppose," Darren said, looking unconvinced.

"Nonsense. The hard part's over, Darren—you've arrived. We'll make it perfect from here."

Out of the corner of her eye, Kelly spied a weary-looking Samantha Douglas coming down the stairs. "Will you excuse me for a moment?"

She dashed over to the writer as she reached the bottom stair. "Did you enjoy your trip to see the falls, Samantha?" Once it looked like the bridal party interview wouldn't happen on time, Kelly had arranged for Bill Williams to take Samantha and her photographer out to frozen Matrimony Falls to see the amazing waterfall that gave the town its name.

"I imagine it's quite stunning when the water's actually flowing."

Kelly had always found the falls to be just as beautiful a sight frozen as in the summer, but she kept that to herself. "It is. Our bride actually considered having an outdoor wedding in front of the frozen falls, but we all decided that was a bit too much of a risk in winter weather."

"Yes," Samantha said coolly. "Winter weather can indeed be risky."

"Not if you're prepared," Kelly countered, "and we are. In fact, our groom and his party just arrived. Why don't you come meet him?"

Before Samantha could object, Kelly waved Bruce, Darren and the other groomsman over to where Samantha was standing. "Darren, this is the writer Bruce told you about from *Southeastern Nuptials*. Samantha Douglas, this is our groom, Darren Billings."

"I had a bit of a time getting here," Darren admitted, "but it looks like I made it to the church on time. Well, the valley at least. Nice to meet you, Ms. Douglas."

"Hello," Samantha said, shaking Darren's hand. "So you're the elk groom."

Kelly cringed. Bruce raised an eyebrow. Darren simply smiled. "I suppose I am. Tina jokes that I would have invited the herd if I could."

"How unusual."

"That's me. Tina sure is tickled you're covering the wedding. When I told her about the interview, she said it made her feel like a celebrity. She's sorry to be missing talking with you today, but I think we've still got time before the wedding. Say, have you ever met an elk, Ms. Douglas?" Darren asked, clearly proud of his life's work. "Such noble creatures."

"Only on the dinner plate, I'm afraid," Samantha replied.

Carly's eyes went wide. "You *eat* them?"

Kelly watched Bruce clamp his hand on Carly's shoulder, surely wishing he could clamp it across her mouth. "Maybe we should head upstairs, Carly."

"But you said I could get ice cream," Carly promptly reminded.

Ice cream? Kelly raised an eyebrow at

Bruce. How had his giving the girls "a talking-to" ended with a promise of ice cream?

"The long trip required a few incentives," Bruce explained with a grimace. He looked down at his daughter. "Why don't we head upstairs for a bit and let Mr. Darren settle in." He looked at Kelly. "We've…um, got a few details to go over, don't we?"

"That we do," she said, still feeling awkward. "Perhaps you could come by the shop after Marvin's? Lulu should be home from school in an hour or so and we can talk about…details…then."

"Am I still in trouble?" Carly asked.

"It's definitely time for us to head upstairs for a bit." Bruce ignored the looks Darren, Samantha and the photographer traded as he turned Carly toward the stairs.

"Everything okay?" Darren asked. "Bruce did seem a bit put out on the drive."

"Everything's fine," Kelly assured. "Samantha, would you like to interview Darren now? I can arrange for his bags to be brought up to his room."

"I wouldn't want to impose after Mr. Billings's long journey," Samantha said.

"No, it's fine. Find me a good cup of coffee and I'll be as good as new. It'll give me something to do while I wait for Tina anyway."

Kelly clapped her hands together. "Great, then, it's settled. Grab those comfy chairs over in the front room and I'll ask Hailey to take care of the rest. Samantha, I'll be back around to escort you over to meet Pastor Mitchell and see the chapel."

Within ten minutes, Darren and Samantha were chatting over coffees in the inn's front room. Kelly fought the urge to stay and supervise, but she was sure Samantha would consider that intrusive. Besides, it wasn't as if she was nervous about what he might say. Darren had loved all the unique preparations, according to Tina, and she was going to have to trust that all that creativity would come through in the interview. And if not the interview, then in the events about to unfold for the wedding.

If everything got the chance to unfold.

Of course it will, Kelly told herself. The groom was in town. The next hurdle to clear was Tina and her parents' safe arrival. Then the guests, then the rehearsal dinner, then the ceremony. One step at a time.

And the next step was talking with Bruce about the valentines. That felt as daunting as any of the wedding tasks. They'd need to correct the girls' thinking without squelching their friendship. Not to mention clearing the air between Bruce and herself so that the wedding didn't get more complicated than it already was. *Ha!* Kelly mused to herself. *Add that to my endless list of tasks.*

She checked the long list on the clipboard she carried as she walked across the street, stepping around the accumulating drifts. At least the snow had tapered off long enough to let Samantha see the falls. Preparations hadn't gone anything close to smoothly, but everything was still moving ahead, and that's what mattered.

Even as she had the thought, a big fat snowflake landed on her paper, melting into a wet ring as two more followed suit. She looked up into the gray-white sky, thick clouds hiding any hint of sun as heavy flakes began to fall all around her.

She sighed. The predicted second wave of snow had begun. *We can still do this*, Kelly told herself as she hugged the clipboard to her chest to protect it from further flakes and dashed for the flower shop door.

An hour later, Bruce pushed open the door of Love in Bloom to finally talk over this sticky situation with Kelly. Not one bit of this vacation was turning out the way he'd planned. Between Kelly, Lulu, Darren and the snow, he was beginning to wonder if the entire wedding was going to be an exercise in adapting to challenges.

"Remember what we talked about," he reminded Carly, who despite a healthy dose of ice cream was dragging her feet reluctantly behind him. A smarter man might have forced the ice cream to wait until after this necessary apology, but he wasn't a smarter man. Not lately.

Carly looked around the shop. "I know I'm s'posed to say I'm sorry to Miss Kelly," she said in a low, slow tone. "And tell her that Lulu and I will mind our own business."

"That's right." He hadn't put it quite so harshly, but Carly's wording did prove she understood how their meddling was wrong.

"What's right?" Kelly came in from the shop's back room.

"We're right here, right after ice cream," Bruce said, wondering what she'd heard.

"Oh," Kelly said. He didn't know if it made him feel better or worse to know she looked as unsettled by this whole business as he did. The entire day seemed to conspire to keep them from discussing it, which just made the anticipation of it worse. What made it worst of all, honestly, was the unnerving notion of a grain of truth to what the girls had done. There really was a—a what? A pull, an attraction, a friendship, a something between him and Kelly. It was just that the timing and circumstances were way off.

"Hello, Carly," Kelly said with a slightly serious tone as she came out from behind the counter.

"Hello, Miss Kelly." Carly stepped forward, evidently summoning her pint-size bravery to get straight to the point. "I'm sorry me and Lulu made those valentines without your—" she scrunched up her face to recall the big word Bruce had used "—permission."

Kelly crouched down to Carly's height. "I see."

"I really like you and Lulu," Carly said, looking right into Kelly's tender eyes. "We were just wishing."

"Wishes are good things," Kelly replied, "but some wishes grown-ups get to make for themselves." Bruce was relieved she kept her gaze on Carly when she said that.

"That's what Daddy said," Carly replied. "And that I hafta say I'm sorry. So I am." She surprised Bruce by asking her, "You'll still let me be flower girl, won't you?" There was a great deal of worry in her tiny voice. To her, it probably made perfect sense that the florist was in charge of the flower girl.

"Oh, sweetheart," Kelly said as she pulled

Carly into a hug. "Of course I will. Darren and Tina chose you to be flower girl, nothing changes that." She pulled back and held Carly's shoulders. "And I accept your apology. What you and Lulu did was wrong, but I am glad to know you like me, because I like you, too, and I want us to be friends."

"What about Dad?"

Kelly straightened. "Your dad and I can be friends, too, but that's up to us, not to little girls sneaking valentines. Understood?"

"Yes, ma'am," Carly said.

"Well, now, I've got something on the counter that you can play with while your dad and I talk, okay?"

He followed Kelly through the archway to her back room, where they could talk while still keeping an eye on Carly happily coloring at the shop counter. She produced her valentine, handing it to him matter-of-factly. "What did yours look like?"

He pulled his version from his jacket pocket and handed it to her, scanning the frilly card she gave him. Even though they were essentially trading evidence of wrongdoing, it still felt peculiar to be standing with this woman exchanging valentines.

"I'm so sorry this happened." It seemed like the right thing for him to say.

"It's not your fault." Her tone was as flustered as his. "It's…well, it's nothing you did. The girls just…dreamed it up, that's all."

Bruce rubbed the back of his neck at the collection of glittery hearts in his hand. "Carly's never done anything like this before. I don't know what to say."

"Lulu hasn't, either. But she will be spending this afternoon writing you an apology note. I've already told her so."

"There's no need," he said. "She apologized—and rather dramatically at that—at breakfast."

"Well, she ought to have."

"I think we can let it drop. By now, they get why what they did was wrong."

Kelly sighed. "She's still writing that letter, because I want her to think long and hard before she tries anything like that ever again. But then, yes, we can all let it go." She picked up a square of green foam from the shelf next to her and began to fiddle with it. "I don't mean that…well, that you're… I mean, you're a perfectly nice man and all but…"

"They were way out of line," Bruce finished for her.

"They just got caught up in the day. We've dealt with it like responsible parents, and now

we can just move on." She was looking anywhere but at him. "There's a lot to do."

"And the second wave of snow's arriving.
This batch is supposed to be worse."

Kelly put a hand to her forehead. "Yes,
there's a snowstorm coming. And Samantha's
watching everything we do."

"Well, I've secured the arrival of the groom.
How else can I help?" Had those words just
left his mouth? Shouldn't he be heading on
back to the safety of the inn rather than offering to spend more time in close proximity
to Kelly Nelson?

He pretended not to notice how anxiously
relieved she looked at his offer. "Well, now
that you mention it, I am in serious need of
someone with long arms."

Twenty minutes later, as Bruce was finishing washing out the last of some tall tin
containers in Kelly's back room, he heard
his daughter call, "Come here, Daddy. Come
look!"

He turned the corner from the back room
to find Carly twirling in the center of the shop
with a wild crown of flowers and ribbons on
her head. She looked just like a princess—if
that princess had an unchecked enthusiasm
for flowers and ribbons. The thing on top of
her head was closer to a parade float than

anything he'd seen in a fairy book. He could barely find her eyes under all the decoration.

"I'm princess of the reindeers!" she declared, twirling one hand in royal splendor.

"That's quite a crown, Your Majesty," he replied, barely containing his laughter as the crown wobbled over her eyes.

"Just 'Your Highness,'" Carly corrected. "Majesty is for kings and queens, and I'm only a princess."

"Oh. Excuse my mistake, Your Highness."

"Miss Kelly is the queen," Carly pronounced, gesturing toward the counter. Bruce followed her gesture to find Kelly arranging pine boughs with an equally silly—but slightly smaller—crown on her own head. Kelly smiled and bobbed a curtsy as if flower shops crowned reindeer queens and princesses every day. Things felt as if they'd returned to the ease between them—mostly.

Bruce returned his gaze to Carly, who seemed to be eyeing his own head with clear plans for further coronations.

"Easy there, Pops," Kelly said, catching his worry. "I suggested an adaptation." From next to her on the counter Kelly produced a makeshift tie fashioned from the red flannel he recognized as Darren and Tina's wedding fabric, only with three large red carnations affixed down the front. Not exactly dignified, but a lot better than what he'd feared given the head-gear of his current companions.

"You may kneel," Carly said in an exceedingly royal manner.

There was nothing to do but lower himself down on one knee and reply, "As you wish, Your Highness," with as much solemnity as he could muster.

"I pronounce you the Reindeer King," Carly declared as Bruce bowed his head for her to slip the decoration over his head with all the pomp of an Olympic medal. "You may rise."

Kelly gave a dignified "golf clap" from her post behind the counter. "Hail, hail, Reindeer King," she said with a chuckle. "With wishes of health and prosperity to both you and your kingdom of my very clean tall vases."

"I made 'em myself," Carly boasted as she pointed to both the tie and her crown. "With a bit of help."

"Not as much as you'd think," Kelly added. "Like I said, she's got quite a knack."

Bruce looked at his tie and the rainbow of shrubbery nearly hiding his daughter's head. "Looks like she's got a whole lot of knack if you ask me."

The bell over the door gave its chime, and a young woman stomped snow off her shoes as she walked into the shop. "Sorry I'm late, Kelly. It's getting nasty out there." She looked up, startled at the floral accessories currently on display. "What's this?"

"Bruce and Carly, this is Cathy Bolton. She watches the shop for me some afternoons."

"Bruce Lohan," Bruce said, remembering his manners despite his current ridiculous appearance.

Cathy pulled off her snowy mittens to shake his hand. With a smirk, she nodded at the tie. "Spiffy neckwear you got there."

"He's the Reindeer King," Carly explained.

Cathy turned and smiled at Carly. "And that makes you…?"

"The Reindeer Princess, of course."

"Of course," Cathy agreed with a laugh.

"And the Flower Queen will now pass the crown to her successor," Kelly said, removing her "crown" and handing it to the young woman. She reached for the clipboard he always saw her carrying and tucked it into a bag. "I need to go get the Elk Princess off her school bus in this blizzard." She handed a list to Cathy. "Here's what still needs to be done for the centerpieces and the pew boughs. And there are two orders for delivery tomorrow, if you can get to them."

"Sure thing," Cathy said, tucking her handbag under the counter and donning the crown with admirable seriousness. "I accept the duties of my crown as bestowed."

"Great."

Bruce went to get his own and Carly's coats, reaching to remove the tie as he did so. "We'll head on back to the inn and see how Darren's doing."

"Oh, no, Daddy. You have to leave the tie on," Carly admonished.

"I do?" He didn't really relish the idea of walking down Aisle Avenue looking like this.

Kelly saved the day. "Carly and I decided that Lulu has to deliver her apology in person just like you did, if you don't mind coming back to the house for a short bit."

"Like this?" He pointed to the tie.

Kelly looked at Carly. "It's pretty messy out. I think we should allow the Reindeer King to zip up his coat, for his own protection and all."

"Oh, yes, of course," Carly agreed.

Bruce zipped up his daughter's coat, carefully pulling her hood over the cascade of ribbons that fell over her back and shoulders. She grabbed another crown off the counter. "I made a crown for Lulu, too."

"That's nice of you." It felt like things had returned to normal between the girls, too. That was good—he wanted the rest of the week to be fun for Carly, and tension between her and Lulu would spoil that.

"Let's go," Kelly said as she pulled open the door. "The other princess will be home in ten minutes if the bus hasn't been delayed by all this snow."

"Have fun storming the castle!" Cathy called.

Bruce caught Kelly's eye over the often-quoted line from one of his and Sandy's favorite movies. *"The Princess Bride?"*

"Cathy babysits for us, so she knows our favorites."

"Princess Buttercup," Carly cried in recognition. "I like her, too!"

"And brave Westley," Kelly added.

"And we can't forget the Dread Pirate Roberts," said Bruce.

"Daddy, can we play snow hopscotch in our crowns once Lulu gets home?"

"As you wish," Kelly and Bruce said in unison. Maybe they had made it over this awkward hump after all.

Chapter Ten

"You'll call if Samantha needs anything? Anything at all?" Kelly had forgotten to check in on Yvonne and her interview with Samantha, so she'd dialed her cell phone as they walked to Lulu's bus stop. Yvonne's sophisticated bakery was perhaps the valley's best shot to impress the *Nuptials* reporter, but Kelly knew too much was riding on this article to leave anything to chance.

"It went great, Kelly. I fed her my black forest cake."

"That secret special icing had to wow her. It did, didn't it?" Nearly every bride who tried Yvonne's black forest cake ordered it—Tina included. The uniquely rich, dark cake hidden under layers of creamy frosting was everyone's favorite. No other cake Kelly had ever tasted came close, even down in Asheville. Just thinking about it made Kelly's mouth water.

"Of course she did. Said she'd never tasted anything like it," Yvonne replied. "Although I could have done without the remark about the surprise of finding something so amazing *all the way out here.* You'd think we were atop the Himalayas the way she talks."

Kelly gulped and looked at the flakes falling all around her. "Let's hope by tomorrow morning we don't *look* like the top of the Himalayas."

"So." Yvonne's tone changed. "There was a certain dad in here with his daughter having a very interesting conversation over cocoa and doughnuts this morning. Not that I was listening in or anything, but your name came up. Repeatedly."

Kelly said a prayer of thanksgiving she hadn't opted for putting the call on speakerphone. "Can we cover this later?"

"Don't deflect. He's very nice, and if his reaction is any indication, the girls definitely picked up on something between the two of you."

"Yvonne, really, can we go over this *another time*?" Struck by inspiration and their location, she added, "I mean, just look out your window."

Bruce, of course, would think she was referring to the snow, but Kelly knew Yvonne's view would clue her in to her present company.

"Oh," Yvonne said. "Now I get it. Hey, good for you. Way to patch things up and get back on track."

That's not the conclusion she wanted Yvonne to draw. Still, there was Yvonne, waving delightedly out the bakery window as they walked past.

Bruce followed her gaze and let out a small but exasperated sigh.

"Everybody wave hello to Yvonne," Kelly called in a falsely cheerful voice as Bruce slanted her a look. Carly, of course, complied with glee, even slipping off her hood to show off the crown and twirling.

Bruce leaned in as he was waving and said, "She knows."

Kelly pointed to the phone. "I know she knows, *now*."

"What? You cut out for a moment," Yvonne said, pointing to her own phone as she stood in the bakery window.

"I will call you later," Kelly said into the phone and then quickly ended the call.

"I like her," Carly offered. "Her doughnuts are good. So are Miss Hailey's waffles.

And Mr. Marvin's ice cream. This whole town is yummy."

"This whole town is nosy," Bruce said under his breath. "I feel like I'm walking in a fishbowl."

Kelly looked up at the sky. "More like a snow globe that just got a good shake." She turned to Bruce. "Tina and her parents will make it in despite all this, won't they?"

Bruce peered up into the parchment-gray skies with an analytical squint. It was dark to the north, even in the middle of the afternoon. He was an experienced pilot, which meant he should be as good at reading the skies as Mark was, shouldn't he? She waited for Bruce to give a reassuring look. He didn't. In fact, he looked downright skeptical as he said, "Last I checked, Darren said they boarded, so they should make it."

"Well, Samantha toured the chapel and left the bakery happy, so there's that." She spied the yellow school bus making the turn onto the street. "And there's Lulu, right on time."

"Lookin' bad," the bus driver called as he pulled open the door. "Doubt I'll be seein' you tomorrow morning. They're sayin' they'll cancel."

Children's cheers rose up from the bus and from Lulu as she made her way down the steps. Her face was a mixture of happiness at seeing Carly and worry at seeing Bruce. Not having heard the conversation Lulu had with Bruce before school, Kelly was glad to see her daughter understood the weight of what she'd done and still felt uneasy about it.

After hugging Kelly and gushing over the flower crowns, Lulu finally dragged her gaze up to Bruce. "Hello, Mr. Bruce." She looked at her mother. "You said I had to write a letter, but I made a card in art instead. Is that okay?"

"Well, I suppose that's all right with me if it's okay with Mr. Bruce." She raised an eyebrow at Lulu. "Even though arts and crafts were kind of how we got into this whole mess to begin with."

"I know," Lulu replied with a pleading expression.

"I'm agreeable," Bruce offered, giving Kelly a look that told her he really wanted this whole episode over with. They both had a lot on their plates in the next few days.

Once they got to the house, Lulu quickly presented Bruce with the "I'm sorry" card and an apology. He read the card, accepted the apology, but still looked as awkward and uncomfortable as she felt. Kelly couldn't escape the feeling that they were both trying very hard to pretend like there was nothing to the girls' assumptions, but were both failing.

"Can Carly stay and play?" Lulu asked, switching gears instantaneously. Clearly, the issue disappeared far faster for the girls than for Bruce and herself.

Bruce checked his watch. "Maybe for half an hour. Then we're due back at the hotel to go with Darren to pick up Tina."

"I'll feel so much better when Tina's here. Everything else can be adapted, but it's mighty hard to have a wedding without a bride."

"I think Darren would agree." The girls skipped off to another part of the house, giggling about their flower crowns, leaving Bruce and Kelly alone in the kitchen.

"Thanks for all the help at the shop today. I mean, you're on vacation. I should have let you spend time with Carly."

"I doubt we'd have done anything she'd have liked as much as flower crowns. I'm not very good at the 'girl fun' stuff, so I'm glad she had the chance." He coughed and shifted his feet. "Actually, on the girl-stuff front, I need some advice."

"On?"

Bruce stuffed his hands in his pockets. "Hair."

He seemed so uncomfortable that Kelly

thought she had to lighten the mood. "I think the touch of gray at your temples is just fine. Distinguished, even." He wasn't gray at all, and it was clear he wasn't asking about his own hair, but someone needed to knock some of that seriousness out of him or they'd never get through this.

He grimaced. "*Her* hair."

Kelly laughed. "I know. Since you're asking, I'd go with a matching headband and maybe a little bit of curling iron the morning of the ceremony."

"I don't have either of those."

"The headband I can fashion from the wedding fabric and ribbons I've got at the shop. And there'll be no shortage of curling irons or hot rollers around the inn the morning of the ceremony. If nothing else I'm sure Hailey can find you one. But really, all you'll likely need to do is wash and brush."

"I think I can handle that." Another long pause where they didn't seem to know what to say to each other.

Kelly was just about to offer to make coffee when her cell phone rang.

"It's Craig from the hardware store," a panicked voice said. "You'd better get over here."

Now what? "Why?" Kelly asked.

"It's that reporter woman. She was over here looking for a cell phone charger or something and she slipped on the sidewalk in front of the store."

Just when she thought things couldn't get worse. "How bad is it?" Her question caught Bruce's immediate attention.

"Rob says we ought to call Doc Merrick." Kelly heard Samantha's sharp voice snap something mean-sounding in the background. "You should really get over here."

"I'll call Doc and be there in five minutes." She ended the call and swiped through her contacts to find Doc Merrick's number. "Samantha slipped on the snow outside the hardware store," she explained to Bruce. "She's hurt."

"That's the last thing anybody needs," Bruce said as Kelly made the call. "Girls," he called, "get your jackets back on!"

"How'd he *do* that?" Bruce said in a stunned whisper to Kelly from the lighting aisle at Rob Folston's Have N Hold Home and Garden store. The two of them were peering through the shelves like teenagers sneaking around a high school library at Rob Folston and Samantha Douglas. Bruce could no more explain what they'd found upon arriving at the store than Kelly could.

"I don't know," admitted Kelly with equal astonishment.

Bruce gave her a puzzled smirk. "I've seen gifted first responders, but this guy has missed his calling in a hardware store."

In the time it had taken him and Kelly and the girls to call the doctor and reach the store, Rob Folston had unpacked a camp chair with an attached footstool, activated one of those crack-to-cool ice packs, opened a package of wooly socks—pink, no less—and erected a spontaneous comfort station into which the man had deposited Samantha.

"I'm not even sure why Craig called me," Kelly said with astonishment in her voice. "Rob has this totally under control. In fact, I think he has it more under control than I ever could."

They watched as Rob handed Samantha a cup of tea and held the woman's hand while Doc Merrick gently examined the ankle in question.

"He's holding her hand," Bruce said. "Do they know each other?"

"I can't imagine they do," Kelly replied, peering around a shelf. She looked at Bruce with a sudden thought. "You don't think she's in shock or something?"

"You'll be just fine," Rob was saying in tones Bruce would never associate with a hardware store. "My sidewalk would never seriously harm a woman as beautiful as you, Ms...."

"Douglas," Samantha said, her voice pitching upward as Doc Merrick seemed to hit a tender spot. Samantha's ankle was already alarmingly swollen, leading Bruce to hope for Kelly's sake it wasn't broken. Sending Samantha Douglas out of Matrimony Valley in an ambulance or a cast seemed like a surefire path to a terrible write-up.

When Samantha added, "But you can call me Samantha," Bruce and Kelly gaped at each other. Kelly had to put her hand over her mouth to squelch an astonished giggle. Today had officially tipped over from stressful to absurd.

"Why are you hiding?" Carly questioned entirely too loudly as she and Lulu came up the aisle shaking seed packets they found somewhere in the store like sets of maracas.

"We're not hiding," Bruce said, stepping away from how close he'd been standing to Kelly.

"You look like you're hiding," Lulu declared.

"We're giving Ms. Douglas some privacy while Doc Merrick sees if her leg is okay," Kelly said.

Carly chose to take matters into her own hands, poking her head around the end of the aisle and shouting, "Is your leg okay?"

Bruce banged his head against the shelf of gutter downspouts while Kelly moaned and covered her eyes.

"I think she'll be fine, little girl. Thank you kindly for asking," Doc Merrick replied in an amused voice without turning around.

"Can this day get any more complicated?" Kelly winced.

On some hideous cue, Bruce's cell pinged an incoming text. "Probably shouldn't ask that," he warned.

Kelly turned to him, alarmed. "Why?"

Bruce looked back at Samantha, now speaking softly with Rob as he handed her a blanket to put around her shoulders. This guy was somehow soothing the unsoothable Samantha Douglas and it looked like this crisis had been resolved—but he was about to throw a bigger wrench into Kelly's plans. He turned his phone screen so she could see. "Tina's stuck in West Virginia until ten o'clock."

She looked like she might cry. Even though there were a hundred reasons why it was the wrong thing to do, Bruce pulled Kelly into a hug. Her important wedding was falling down around her. He was worried for Darren's big day, surely, but a rebellious part of his heart was aching for the brave and determined woman trying to make that day perfect for herself and a town that desperately needed a boost.

She resisted for a second, a wary look in her eyes, but then fell against him with an enormous exhale. He'd had scores of hugs from concerned friends and family over the past two years, had snuggled countless times with Carly's arms wrapped around his neck, but this was different. The potent shock of a woman in his arms was an extraordinary sensation. And he felt it—perhaps more intently than he'd felt anything in years. A welcome thaw and a bolt of terror at the same time. *Let go*, his brain yelled while his body paid no attention.

…Until the giggles of two little girls made him and Kelly step away from each other at lightning speed.

As it turned out, things could get a whole lot more complicated indeed.

Chapter Eleven

What just happened?

Bruce tried to shake his confusion loose as he watched Kelly and Lulu trudge across the snow-covered street back to the flower shop. His own thoughts seemed to whirl like the flakes around him.

They'd shot apart the minute they'd become aware of the girls' watching them, and then went through an absurd display of denial before maneuvering Samantha Douglas safely back to the inn as if the hug had never happened. The obvious—if baffling—flirtation happening between the writer and Rob Folston just made everything more bizarre.

The last hour had felt ridiculous and exhausted him enough to bring him to do something he tried never to do: plop Carly down in front of the television watching cartoons.

Of course, she'd rather be playing with Lulu, but being anywhere near Kelly Nelson right now felt beyond his ability to cope.

Cope with what? For all his dislike of his previous emotional fog, it was better than the way he felt right now. Numb was much less messy, asked less of him than whatever this was. He needed hours, days, a space the size of the Grand Canyon to sort all this out, and instead he was shackled to his role in a crazy Matrimony Valley elk wedding that was still missing its bride.

When the knock came on his door, he almost didn't answer it. Kelly's pushy nature surely wouldn't let her leave him be after what had happened. She'd want to talk about it, and that was the last thing he wanted to do.

"Dad," Carly called from her spot on the floor in front of the television. "There's someone at the door." There was no avoiding life with a five-year-old watching your every move.

Darren stepped into the room when Bruce opened the door. "You want the good news or the bad news?" the groom asked.

"Good news," Carly answered for him.

"Tina and her parents got on a flight."

"What's the bad news?" Bruce asked.

"It isn't direct, and they land in Charlotte."

That was a drive, but doable.

"At two o'clock in the morning."

Bruce grimaced. "Well, that's lousy, but at least they'll arrive."

Darren stuffed his hands in his pockets. "Yeah, about that. They're all together—which is better than the separate flights we thought they might have to take—but my truck…"

Bruce could all too easily see where this was heading.

"Besides, you've got the only truck with a real back seat, and we need to seat five," Darren said, raising one pleading eyebrow.

"Five?" One groom, one bride and two future in-laws made four. Unless…

"You're not going to make me do this alone, are you? Tina's mother in a good mood is challenge enough. Her mom, and dad, and her after the day they've had? I'd never make it back here alive."

Bruce stared at his friend, wondering just what part of the best man protocol included middle-of-the-night rescue missions.

"Who'll look after Carly?" he asked Darren.

Carly had a ready answer for that question. "I can sleep over at Lulu's! Oh, Dad, it'd be so much fun."

Darren shrugged. "Problem solved."

When Bruce looked unconvinced, Darren continued. "C'mon, you gotta help me. Tina and her folks got the last three seats on what may be the last plane for hours. If I don't pick her up—believe me—there won't be a wedding. And they won't bicker if you're with me. I mean it, man, don't make me do this alone."

"Pleeeeaaaassseee, Daddy? Can I? Can I? I know Lulu's mom will say yes. She likes you a lot."

That last remark brought a questioning glance from Darren, which Bruce shut down with a dark look he didn't have to work at all to call forth. And he'd just watched Kelly head back to Love in Bloom, so he didn't even have the flimsy excuse of not having the florist's home phone number.

Some days the world just ganged up on you without asking permission.

Five minutes later, Bruce swore he could hear Lulu's squeal of delight clear across the avenue. "We'll be happy to host Carly for the night," Kelly said. "Anything to get Tina safely into town."

I really should be asleep.

Kelly shut the door silently after checking on the girls a second time. She told herself she was worried Carly would wake up in the middle of the night and get scared in the unfamiliar surroundings. Then again, Carly had Lulu close by. The girls had become instantly inseparable. *Like sisters*, Kelly couldn't help thinking, wild as that thought was.

Wrapping her robe tighter against the growing howl of the wind outside, Kelly padded downstairs to make herself a soothing cup of herbal tea. The staccato tap of freezing rain against the kitchen windows told her the temperature had indeed warmed up just enough to turn the snowstorm into a more dangerous ice storm. *More dangerous.* Kelly hated how those words planted themselves in her head and dug under her composure.

She was worried about Tina's safe arrival in this threatening weather, but another thought niggled at her brain, too—what had happened in the aisles at Rob's hardware store. It was as if she'd somehow convinced her body to forget what it was like to fall into a man's strong arms, and today had woken up the memory. And now she remembered what she was missing. And she *did* miss it. Fiercely. How was it possible that tonight, after all this time of coming to terms with being alone, she felt more alone than ever?

An unwelcome worry over Bruce, out on

the road in this storm with Darren, chewed at her. She wasn't overreacting; it was dangerous on the roads. *Keep them safe and get them here*, she prayed as she heated water in the microwave.

Middle-of-the-night "keep him safe" prayers. Oh, what familiar territory this was. An old wound long scarred over. Scars were supposed to be tougher and less sensitive than unmarked skin, but that worked only with bodies, not souls. Being in the kitchen in the middle of the night with one small light on, a prayer in her heart and a cup of herbal tea in her hands—this was a posture she knew all too well.

She'd always worried over Mark, even before Lulu's arrival made those fears more acute. *I'm safer than every car on the road*, he would always tell her. Statistically, she knew that to be true. Only the facts had never stopped the worry—and neither the facts nor the worry had saved Mark. To this day, bad weather could send her pulse skyrocketing on sheer remembered fear alone.

Think about possibilities, not problems, she told herself. Years from now, Darren and Tina would tell the story of how the snowstorm threatened their wedding but how it came off beautifully in the end. There'd be jokes about how smart it was for the bride to dress her attendants in flannel and boots, how the sun outside the church reflected off the drifts of fresh snow.

How a single patch of ice could reduce the weekend to tragedy. *You never know. You can never know.*

Bruce had brushed off the danger of the drive with the same confidence Mark always exhibited. *I know what I'm doing,* he'd said in reply to her *Be careful!* admonition on his way out the door. She believed he did know what he was doing, but so did Mark. She shook her head, trying to shake the way her thoughts were meshing the two men together. While they refused to say it, she and Bruce both knew the girls hadn't made things up out of thin air; there was a genuine attraction brewing between Bruce and her.

Bruce's circumstance and his profession, however, were clear red flags warning her off. Sign on for a second tour of middle-of-the-night worries? No, sir. Not for anything or anyone.

"Mom?"

She turned to find a sleepy-eyed Lulu leading a teary-eyed Carly down the stairs.

"The storm is scaring Carly."

Not just Carly, Kelly thought as she came

toward the girls and gathered both of them in a big hug. "Let's come snuggle on the couch and I'll relight the fire."

"Where's Daddy?" Carly said, sniffling.

"He's with Darren picking up Tina and her parents at the airport. Do you remember?"

"Oh." Her tiny voice was a mixture of tearful whine and sleepy yawn.

"Your daddy is being very brave and helpful. After all, we need our bride, don't we?"

When the three of them had settled into a cozy trio on the couch in front of the fire, Lulu looked up into Kelly's eyes. "Is the storm bad?"

As if responding to her question, a burst of freezing rain scattered ominous *tap-tap-taps* across the living room window. "It should be fine by morning," Kelly reassured, even though she wasn't sure of that at all. "But I think your bus driver is right. I doubt you'll have school tomorrow."

"Oh, goody," Lulu said, snuggling in closer. "Carly and I can play together all day then, can't we?"

"That'd be fun," said Carly, who was now half-asleep against Lulu in the most heartwarming pile of girls and blankets Kelly had ever seen. *Well, if I'm going to be up, I can't think of a better place to be than right here.*

She reached out and brushed the hair out of each girl's face, marveling at the perfection of closed eye lashes fluttering against each pink cheek.

"Mmm." Carly sighed at the touch, her eyes fluttering open for a moment to focus with uncertainty on Kelly. "Mom?"

Kelly's heart twisted. Carly couldn't have been more than three when her mother died. Did she have a clear memory of her mother anymore? She knew it haunted Bruce, the way keeping Mark alive for Lulu weighed on Kelly's mind.

"Your mama's in heaven, darling," Kelly replied, the words barely making it past the lump that rose in her throat. "Looking down on you and smiling wide." It was what she told Lulu all the time; that Mark looked down and rejoiced over the girl she was becoming.

"Not here." For their simplicity, Carly's words held the whole weight of the problem. Lots of things weren't here. Heaven was far away, and lives still had to be lived here, where people were gone and not everything worked the way it should. Where little girls woke up in the middle of the night without mommies and daddies.

"No, sweetheart, but I'm glad to be here." She was. There was something about Carly that had latched onto Kelly's heart and refused to let go. She enjoyed all the bridal parties, took pleasure in the steady stream of new people who came to Matrimony Valley for weddings. It was the best of both worlds—old reliable friends and new visitors. But Carly? She couldn't quite say how Carly was different, only that she was.

"Daddy?" Carly roused again, looking around the space.

"He's off to get Miss Tina, remember?" When Carly looked a little alarmed, she added, "He'll be just fine."

He'll be just fine. She'd said that to Lulu the stormy night Mark did not come back. A perfectly ordinary promise to make to a child, and the worst one in the world not to keep.

The wind howled against the windows again, tugging at the frayed edge of her confidence that all would truly be well. If the doubt pulled too hard, that frayed edge threatened to unravel.

She couldn't unravel again. She wouldn't survive it. A life alone, sustained by memories, was far better than ever risking anything like the shattering loss of Mark again. And the impact would not only affect her—she couldn't bear the thought of Lulu growing up thinking everyone you loved died and left you alone.

Kelly closed her eyes and told her pulse to remember that God hadn't taken His eyes off her, Lulu or even the whole of Matrimony Valley. *Help me remember how grateful I am for all You've done here*, she prayed. Mark could always remind her how gratitude was the best antidote to her controlling nature. *Oh, how I miss your wisdom and love, Mark.*

She let herself admit it for the first time in a long time: *I'm lonely. I'm capable, I'm independent, but I'm lonely.*

There. She'd said it—silently, yes, but even that felt like a monumental shout into the shimmering sleet as it slanted down to complicate her life. *I'm lonely. Everything is stretching me lately, and it would be so nice to have someone to lean on.*

She did, of course. She had a sovereign God, good friends, her own parents and even Mark's.

None of those blessings counterbalanced the startling ache that rose up when Bruce Lohan stepped back after holding her. Someone else who knew the size and shape of the gaping hole Mark had left in her life. Who understood the particular endurance required to hold it together for a child's benefit even while you felt your world was being ripped in a dozen pieces. The sadness in his eyes somehow reminded her she wasn't truly happy. Coping, yes. Succeeding—that was definitely in progress. Content? Most days.

But truly, profoundly happy? The actual deep truth was that she didn't think that kind of happiness could be hers again. Mark would tell her to be grateful she'd had it at all, wouldn't he? She could name several people who'd had nothing near the happiness she and Mark had known.

She knew better than to think any one life was more protected than another—people died in their beds asleep, healthy people suddenly took ill, lives ended in all kinds of unexpected and unpreventable ways. But to walk *toward* risk, to invite it back in when it had done such massive damage already? No, she couldn't do that. Ever.

So why was the color of Bruce's eyes the last thing she remembered as she drifted off to sleep?

Chapter Twelve

The insistent knocks startled Kelly awake. It took her a second to recognize where she was and who was under the two lumps of blankets beside her on the couch. Bits of pink were just poking their way through parchment-gray skies. A set of knocks came again to the front door.

As quickly as she could, Kelly extracted herself from the mound of blankets. The girls roused a bit, but settled back into sleep as she rushed to the door and saw a worried Bruce peering through the glass.

"I've sent half a dozen texts," he said loudly until she put her finger to her lips and nodded toward the couch. "You didn't answer." He added a weary glare to his insistent whisper.

"I was at the counter when the girls came down in the middle of the night. I must have left the phone over there while we all slept on the couch." Her neck pinched from the awkward sleeping arrangements. Today was going to be tough enough without the ravages of a poor night's sleep.

Bruce's eyes widened. "Up in the middle of the night? Was Carly scared?"

Kelly yawned and ran her hands through what must be a tumble of her hair. "More like confused. Once I reminded her where you were and that you'd be fine, she and Lulu conked out on the couch with me. They slept like babies. Me—" she yawned "—not so much." Remembering his vital mission, she added, "You made it there and back okay?"

Bruce winced. "We made it there and back. 'Okay' remains to be seen."

"What do you mean? Is Tina here?" She pulled a bag of coffee grounds from the kitchen cabinet and raised it toward him in a "want some?" gesture, to which he nodded.

"Remember when I said Tina was a laid-back kind of bride?"

"I do."

"She's not. Well, not anymore. I think she was grateful we drove two and a half hours in a storm to get her from the airport, but that gratitude was buried under two and a half hours of worried arguing with her parents and

Darren for the whole ride back." He sank onto the stool, rolling shoulders that looked as sore as Kelly felt. "I felt like the truck cab shrank with every mile. I was glad to help Darren out, but by thirty minutes west of Charlotte I was wishing I'd convinced him to just take my keys and leave me here."

"Oh, dear." Kelly laughed softly as she scooped grounds into the coffeepot. "That sounds tense."

"Yeah." Bruce yawned. "You can say that again. You might not want to let those two anywhere near Samantha today."

Samantha. In all the worry over the bride and groom she'd forgotten about Samantha, her injury and the long-postponed interview she supposed Samantha expected to happen now that Tina had arrived. "Well, maybe everyone will be in better spirits after a few hours' sleep." She pressed the button to start the brewing, only to have the lights flicker. *No. No, no, no.* A power outage was the absolute last thing anyone needed. It still wasn't light enough to make out anything in the backyard. "How bad is it out there?"

"Not good. Things are pretty iced over. Tina said the airline told her they were the last flight in—cancellations were piling up fast." The lights flickered again, and Bruce looked at her. "I don't think anyone else who's flying in today is going to make it. And I'm not so sure about anyone driving, either."

"It's got to clear up between now and the wedding, right?" What a foolish question. The weather reports she'd been trying to ignore all told her the storm wouldn't let up anytime soon. As if they had heard her question, the lights flickered again and then went out. The coffee maker halted midprocess. A lot of things halted.

"Lord have mercy." Kelly sighed, thinking mercy and grace would be needed in gigantic proportions today. She salvaged the tiny amount of coffee that had made it into the carafe and poured it out into two meager half-mug portions. The first part of the pot was always stronger than she liked, but she'd need all the caffeine she could manage today. "This won't be enough."

Bruce took the mug and downed it in one gulp. "It's a start."

The house phone rang, startling the girls awake. "It must be five forty-five," Kelly said, reaching for the receiver. "That's when they call to cancel school."

"Mom?" Lulu's voice came from the couch.

"Dad?" came Carly's voice right behind.

"Here," Kelly and Bruce said in unison. It struck an odd note with everyone.

She hadn't even hung up on the recorded "school is canceled" call when Carly and Lulu cheered "No school!" in unison. Things were "pairing off" far too fast in this impromptu foursome.

"So can we make pancakes?" Lulu asked with wide eyes. Why was it children had such a talent for being wide awake on days parents would have dearly loved them to sleep in? Kelly was drowsy, Bruce was exhausted, but Carly and Lulu had apparently found boundless energy despite the early hour.

Kelly opted for surrender. "Have you eaten?"

Bruce made a face. "Does gas station food count?"

She could just imagine what had passed for middle-of-the-night sustenance on Bruce's bridal-recovery mission. "I don't think so."

"Do you put chocolate chips in your pancakes?" Carly asked as she got up off the couch and planted herself expectantly on one of the two kitchen stools.

"Mom puts bananas in ours." Lulu looked up at Kelly with a sweet face and wide eyes. "But I think bananas and chocolate chips go really well together. Don't you, Mom?"

Kelly offered her daughter a look. "I think you two girls are getting just a little too good at scheming together."

"Banana chocolate chip pancakes." Carly said the words with such relish Kelly knew she'd be unable to resist.

"Well, maybe they can't cook without electricity," Bruce said, clearly offering her the only available out.

"Oh, no. Our stove is gas. Only our fridge and lights don't work when the power's out. And the fireplace can keep us warm, too."

"Miss Kelly has a complicated day ahead of her, Carly. She may not have time to be making a big breakfast for us when we should be able to get something at the inn."

"But their power's out, too, right, Mom?" Lulu replied. "And you always say a big day needs a big breakfast." Both girls began enthusiastically nodding their endorsement of the idea.

Kelly looked at Bruce. "It is going to be a big day. Big victory or big problem, or both— it'll definitely be big."

Another burst of icy rain struck the kitchen windows, and the brightening daylight showed an alarming frosting of ice on everything in sight. "Big storm, that's for sure," he said with a worry she felt pressing down her own shoulders. "You got a woodpile?"

"By the rental cabin back behind the garage, but I'm not sure how much of it is split. It's not exactly how I choose to get my exercise."

"But you've got an ax?"

"There's one back there, yes."

He put his hat back on his head and grabbed his gloves off the hall table. "I'll get you set for wood while you get the girls set for breakfast."

She couldn't help but be grateful for the assistance. The logs that were split out in the shed wouldn't last long if the fireplace had to be going nonstop to keep the house warm. "Thanks."

"Hooray!" Lulu and Carly cheered.

Bruce was just finishing the last load of wood when his cell phone went off in his pocket.

"You left thirty minutes ago. Where are you?" Clearly Darren hadn't been able to fall into bed as planned.

"I'm at Kelly Nelson's house, where Carly spent the night. What's up?"

"The power's out."

"I'm aware of that. I'm over here getting

Kelly set for wood in case they need it. Everything okay over there?"

Bruce heard Tina yelling something in the background. "What do you think?"

Suddenly, Kelly Nelson's house was looking like the most peaceful place imaginable to have breakfast. "Tina's not too happy about the storm, huh?"

"You could say that."

Understatement of the year, Bruce thought to himself. Tina's fuse had grown so short by the time they'd returned to Matrimony Valley Bruce hadn't even bothered to try to go up to his room at the inn. Those four—Darren, Tina and Tina's parents—were a barrel of stress he didn't need. Best man duties went only so far, and he'd already gone above and beyond. "Well, hang tight, maybe get some breakfast, and I'll see you once Carly's done with breakfast over here."

"Flights are canceled for hours," Darren said quietly—but not quietly enough to keep his bride from overhearing.

"Hours!" Tina moaned in the background. "No one's going to get here, are they?"

"Maybe not, sweetheart," Darren said carefully. He used the voice of a man defusing a bomb. A bridal bomb poised to go off any moment. Chocolate chip banana pancakes were looking better by the minute.

He felt like he had to ask. "You gonna be okay over there?"

"That remains to be seen."

"She's going to be your wife tomorrow. You might as well learn to handle her in a mood now. Besides, this will make a great story to tell the grandkids."

"Darren, will you get off the phone with Bruce and help me figure out what to do about this?" came Tina's sharp voice over the line. Bruce winced, and suspected his friend was doing the same.

"For the record, this will only make a great story to tell the grandkids *if we actually get married and have kids*," Darren whispered.

"Sun's not even fully up yet. You've got loads of time to make this work." He should have said "we've got," but at the moment he was grateful for every foot of icy snow between him and the irritated bride. "Godspeed, man."

Even as he clicked off the line, Bruce could hear Tina's raised voice and sharp tone. A guilty chuckle rumbled up from his chest as he hoisted the last of the split logs and made his way to Kelly's back door.

The most delicious scent met him as Carly pulled the door open. The house smelled warm and sweet, slightly smoky and sugary and altogether cozy. The exact opposite of whatever strife Darren was currently wrangling.

As he deposited the wood by the roaring fire and shucked his coat, he called a warning to Kelly. "Your bride's in full-scale meltdown, by the way."

"Is she?" Kelly slid a plate of steaming pancakes in front of Carly, who grinned from ear to ear. The pancakes he served usually came from a box in the freezer. This homemade batch looked as delicious as they smelled.

"That bit you said about even the calmest bride getting a little nuts? Sounds like Tina left 'a little nuts' behind an hour ago."

"You better have a double helping, Mom," Lulu cautioned as she dug into the plate Kelly had just set before her. Bruce had to admit, he was looking forward to digging into a plate of his own—the food and atmosphere here had to be ten times better than whatever was happening back at the inn.

"I'll admit, today presents some challenges." She used the delicate tone of someone trying hard to put the best possible spin on a fast-degrading situation. "But it's still early. A lot can still go right."

"Or wrong," Lulu said with a mouthful of pancake.

"Can Miss Tina and Mr. Darren still get married?" Carly asked. "Will I still get to wear my dress and boots?"

Bruce thought he ought to leave that one to the professional, so he said nothing.

Kelly leaned down on the countertop so that her face was at Carly's height. "A wedding only needs four things to happen. Do you know what those are?"

"What?"

"A bride, a groom, a minister and God. Mr. Darren is here. Miss Tina just got here. Pastor Mitchell's always been here, and God is everywhere. So we're set. Everything else is just nice extras."

That sounded awfully simplistic for the "gotta get it perfect" florist Kelly had been since he'd met her. Did she really believe that? Or was she just pep-talking herself along with Carly?

Carly, who was now pouting. "I'm just extra?"

Bruce had been indulging her by telling her what an important part of the wedding she was. "That makes me an extra, too," he told her. "But we're extra-important extras now, because we're here." He nodded toward the window. "And maybe not everyone will be able to get here now."

"So we have to be extra enough for everybody?"

"We might," Kelly replied, not exactly keeping all the worry out of her tone. She looked at Bruce. "One of the bridesmaids lives close, right?"

"The maid of honor."

"And the other groomsmen—two live within an hour's drive, if I remember?"

He shrugged. "Well, an hour's drive on a good day. They were supposed to come in for a campfire tonight, but now…who knows?"

"The groomsmen's campfire at the cabin. I always thought that was such a nice touch. And now…" She put one hand on her forehead. Her brain was flying a mile a minute, he could see it in her eyes.

"Kelly…"

"No, really, it'll be fine. We'll make it work. We'll…"

"No, Kelly, the pancakes…" He gestured to the smoke rising from the griddle behind her.

"Yikes!" she cried, whirling so fast she knocked the jar of maple syrup off the counter. Bruce lunged to catch it, but missed, and it hit the floor with a thick-sounding crack.

"Oh, no!" Lulu cried as the broken jar began oozing syrup across the floor.

"Ouch!" Kelly yanked her hand back from the griddle pan where she had grabbed it without a hot pad in her surprise.

The next ten seconds were a flurry of yelps, winces, shouts and grabs as Bruce used a towel to move the smoking pan off the burner, threw a second towel over the sticky mess on the floor, kept the barefooted girls on their stools and away from the broken glass and shifted Kelly to the sink.

"I'm going to need this hand," she moaned as she flexed her red fingers and palm under the running water. "And now there's no more syrup for pancakes. The rehearsal dinner is tonight, the wedding is tomorrow…" She swallowed and looked up at the ceiling, blinking hard. Bruce's stomach knotted. He couldn't hug her again in front of the girls—it would just make everything worse. But so much of him wanted to.

At a loss for how to comfort her, he put a hand on her shoulder while she sucked on the pad of her burned thumb, one tear slipping down her cheek.

It was a mistake. Touching her, even on the

shoulder, seemed to intensify the feelings already edging out of his control. Parts of him kept closing the space between them—literally and emotionally—without his permission.

She shifted her head to look at him, and it was all there in her eyes. The pileup of worry, the nonstop struggle to get by, the importance she'd heaped onto this wedding, the desperate cling to independence he knew so well. Why did he feel like he understood her on such a deep level when they'd known each other less than a week? She was the florist for a wedding he was standing up for—why wouldn't it stay just that?

"Mom, are you okay?" came Lulu's worried voice from behind him.

"It just stings," Kelly said, shutting her eyes even as a second tear slipped down her cheek. *It just stings.* Bruce found the description all too accurate. "Stay where you are, sweetie," she called, forcing her voice to brighten. "Don't get off that stool until we get this glass cleaned up."

As he bent down to the mess on the floor, Bruce wondered if the "we" in Kelly's command stuck with her as much as it did with him.

Chapter Thirteen

"Six more hours?" Kelly watched Hailey slump against the inn's kitchen wall as she held the phone to her ear. "I can't run an inn full of people without power for that long. I barely made it through breakfast and the hot water's all but gone."

Kelly scribbled *Watson's Diner—sandwiches?* on the clipboard that hadn't left her hands in hours. The papers that kept hosting an ever-growing list of tasks and challenges. She was starting to feel like a general on the battlefield. How Mayor Jean handled wedding planning all year long on top of running the Matrimony Valley community was beyond her.

Of course, Mayor Jean never tried to coordinate a wedding in the middle of a snow-and-ice storm. Jean had already called and offered to come over to help in any way she could, but the last thing Kelly wanted was to be worrying about a pregnant and nauseated mayor slipping on her bad ankle on a patch of ice. Couldn't just one of today's problems be uncomplicated?

Hailey hung up the phone. "The county power company says we might get power back on by eight tonight. Might? We need power back on before the rehearsal dinner. We need power back on before *lunch*."

"I know." Kelly sighed. Tina and Darren were impatiently waiting for word that some—even half—of their wedding guests would be able to arrive. And then there was the reporter waiting to cover a wedding that might not happen. "Has anyone seen how Samantha is doing this morning?"

Hailey wiped her bangs out of her eyes. "How should I know? I'm still trying to figure out how to keep the second floor warm."

The second floor, where all the wedding guests were staying. Astonishingly, six guests had actually made it to the valley, but the tales they told of icy roads and closed highways didn't hold out much hope for others arriving anytime soon.

"I can't put it off any longer. Lulu, honey, stay here with Hailey while I go find out just how happy our happy couple still is. Bruce said Tina's nerves are strung a bit thin." That was putting it mildly.

"You can say that again," Hailey muttered. "And who can blame her?"

"It's hopeless," Lulu proclaimed with eight-year-old drama.

"No," Kelly cautioned, "we can't say that. We can think it, we can worry, but we've got to stay positive in how we talk to the guests. To everyone. Come on, girls, we can pull this off. I know we can." Kelly heard the words coming out of her mouth, but she wondered if anyone could see how little she believed them.

"The 'before party' is supposed to be tonight," Carly said as Bruce tried to get her to take a nap back in their room. She hadn't gotten enough sleep last night—and he'd barely had any—so they both needed to rest if tonight had any hope of being fun.

If tonight had any hope of being *at all*.

"Did God send that big awful storm?" she asked as she rolled over to look out the window.

Where had that come from? "Well, now, that's a big question for a little girl," he said, grasping for an answer. "God created the earth, and the sun and stars and winds, so I guess you can say He creates weather. But I don't think He set out to ruin Miss Tina and Mr. Darren's wedding, if that's what you're thinking. I think they'll still get married tomorrow, don't you?"

"We've got the four things Miss Kelly said we needed, don't we?"

He was impressed Carly remembered. Together, they ticked them off on Bruce's fingers. "A bride, a groom, a minister and God." He felt a bit silly boiling down a wedding to those simplistic terms, but he supposed he did believe what the florist said was true—sort of. Life felt anything but simple and God-sent these days. These *years*.

"Did you have those things when you married Mommy?"

Bruce's memory cast back to the sunny fall day he'd made Sandy his wife. He did feel as if God had smiled down on his life that day. The world was filled with possibilities and adventures, and he felt blessed to have such an incredible woman by his side for life.

It was just that "life" hadn't lasted nearly as long as either of them had planned. The "till death do us part" phrase rang ominous in his ears these days, and he wondered if those fateful words would be part of Darren and Tina's vows tomorrow. "We had those things, sweetheart," he answered his daughter. "And we had more. We had electricity, and nice weather, and all our friends could come celebrate with us."

"Did God know I was coming?"

It took him a minute to work out what she meant. "Mommy and I asked God to bless us with children, so yes. You know Mommy always called you her gift from God."

"Did God know Mommy was going away when she did?"

She asked the weighty question with such an innocence it made his heart twist. Bruce sat down on the bed. "What makes you ask that?"

"Mr. Darren told me yesterday that he was sad God called Mommy home before she could be here to watch him marry Miss Tina. But she isn't home, she's in heaven. Did God know that would happen like He knew the storm would happen? Or the storm that took Lulu's daddy away?"

Wow—he was in way over his head. Sandy was always so much better at the hard questions. Bruce thought for a moment, smoothing down Carly's wild hair while he groped for an answer. "I see it this way—God always knows what's happening to us, and He's around to help us. Sometimes that's hard to see, especially when things feel sad or wrong.

Like all of the people who can't get here right now to come to the wedding. That feels sad, and wrong, and it's okay to feel disappointed about it. But it doesn't mean God's not watching over us, or that He isn't in the sad or hard places."

Even as the words left his mouth, Bruce wondered if he still believed them. He'd be lying if he said he didn't continually tamp down a boiling anger at God for taking Sandy from him. That's not what he wanted Carly to learn about God, but he didn't want to hand her platitudes he didn't feel, either. His brain accepted the fact that God could still be found in the sad or hard places. His gut told him that he'd stopped looking for God in those places. That thought woke up the startling notion that given how sad and hard his last two years had been, it meant he'd stopped looking for God altogether.

Were his fog and the lack of God connected? Bruce wasn't sure he was ready to think about that right now. He settled on an answer to satisfy Carly even if he didn't have one to satisfy himself. "I know God will be there tomorrow for Tina and Darren. Even if a whole bunch of things go wrong."

Carly stuck her chin out. "But they won't.

Ms. Kelly said that everything that could go wrong already has."

Bruce wasn't quite sure that was true. A lot could still go wrong in the next twenty-four hours. "What I know, little girl, is that things will go a lot better if you and I get some rest before tonight's party." He settled her back into her blankets and handed her the pink bear that was her bedtime companion. "Can you do that for me?"

"I'll try." The yawn she gave with the words told him Carly would succeed.

Much better than he would. Bruce shut the door partway and sunk into the comfy chair in his adjoining room. *Catch a nap of your own*, he commanded himself. Despite the tiring drive, and even chopping Kelly's wood, he knew it wouldn't work. His brain was in too much of a tangle over Carly's big questions, the threatened wedding and the pretty florist who wouldn't leave his thoughts.

He wasn't ready to let someone else into his life—he knew that. But he also knew how bone-weary he was of being alone. He'd felt less alone in Kelly's kitchen this morning than he'd felt in months. As if he'd been sitting in a dark room and someone struck a match. Just one match, but it was enough to let him see things he wasn't sure he was ready to see.

Bruce laughed at himself. He wasn't a guy for metaphors—that had been Sandy. *The only match you need to worry about right now is Darren's match with Tina. You've got to help find a way for this wedding to happen.*

I've not asked for much, Lord, Bruce found himself praying. *In fact, I've not asked for anything. Or even paid attention to You lately. I didn't see the point when all I'd do is complain. But seeing as weather seems to be Your department, could You step in here? Reduce the catastrophe factor by even a little?*

He doubted God would suddenly lend an ear to the crisis pleas of a man who'd abandoned church until this weekend. Still, maybe the fact that he was asking on someone else's behalf would earn him a shred of attention from the Almighty. Surely God was on the side of happy marriages.

Carly made a small, sleepy noise, and he glanced through the barely open door to see her small figure shift under the blankets.

Thank You for her. I'd never have made it without Carly. I'm not sure I'm making it now, but she's such a gift to me.

Even as a baby, he'd loved watching her sleep. The way her eyelashes fluttered, the rosy curve of her cheek, the way her little pink mouth always hung just a little bit open, the way one hand still clutched the pink bear Sandy had picked out for her first birthday. *When I look at her like this, I can believe You'll let her turn out okay.* He could cling to the hope that the gaping hole in her heart would heal faster than the one in his. *Dear God, let her grow up into someone Sandy would be proud of.*

I don't know how to do this.

He'd said those exact words one night during Carly's first fever as he and Sandy stayed up the whole night.

No one knows how to do this, Sandy had said. *Everyone's just making it up as they go along.*

So make it up as you go along. Bruce picked up the receiver for the monitor he'd been wise enough to pack so he could venture down the hall while she slept. Sleep wasn't going to happen. So he might as well buck up and go see how Darren was faring. If nothing else, he could tell the groom-to-be that any first year of marriage ought to feel easy after the strain it was taking them to actually *get* married.

Bruce wasn't ten feet outside his room when he turned to see Kelly slumped in a hallway chair just down the way from Darren's and Tina's rooms. Her hands covered her eyes. Bruce started to ask, "Are you okay?" but swallowed the question. A sniff and a shuddering breath told him she'd finally given in to the tears she'd fought back earlier this morning. He could see without asking that she wasn't anything close to okay—the whole event was falling down around her. She heard his approach and looked up, clearly upset at his discovery of her at such a loss.

"Tina's sobbing," she said, waving a soggy tissue in the direction of the rooms he'd been approaching. "Our bride's in there crying."

Bruce knew he ought to say something like "It'll be okay," but that seemed trite given the circumstances. Instead, he sat down next to her and put his hand on her shoulder the way he had done this morning. "Sometimes, the weather wins. Not the war, just the battle. Darren and Tina know you can't control that. They know you're trying."

"I am," Kelly groaned as she wiped her eyes. "It was going to be perfect."

Bruce leaned back. "Now it'll just have to be a different kind of perfect. Come on, we know how to do that, you and I. We've been having to create a different kind of perfect for our families since…you know." He groped for some good news, any shred to cheer her up. "Carly's still excited for tonight. She told me it's been her best vacation ever."

"I don't see how," Kelly muttered.

"No, really. Somehow you and Lulu have made this all a grand adventure for her instead of the fiasco I know it feels like to you. I should thank you for that."

She gave a low laugh. "You can't honestly tell me this turned out to be the vacation you planned."

He laughed, as well. "No, you're right there. But somehow, it's fitting the bill of what we really needed. We've had fun." When she looked at him, he amended, "Odd fun, unexpected fun, but fun. If the goal was memories, we're definitely making 'em." After a moment, he hit upon the news he knew would bolster her spirits. "Carly told me she saw a unicorn this morning. An ice unicorn. New species, evidently. She gave a very detailed description, and you should have seen her smile while she did."

Kelly tucked her hair behind her ear. He liked the way it curved around her cheek when it wasn't behind her ear. It framed her face in a simple way that suited her. Shiny and straight, but bouncy and full of movement. "Does that whole business baffle you? Her imaginary unicorns?"

"Sure it does. But I also figure it's her way of telling me she'll be okay. She seems to see it as Sandy telling *her* she'll be okay, and since it's her own imagination, I see it as her telling *me*." He shifted his weight on the small, fussy chair—most of the inn's furnishings felt too small and fussy for him at his size. "It makes me feel better to know she's seen one, because they seem to stop coming when she's sad or bothered."

"Well, then, bring them on. In fact, can we send a herd of those 'feel better' unicorns Tina's way?"

Bruce laughed. "Wasn't that the original plan? Well, elk anyway." They had, in fact, planned to take some of the wedding photos out by the elk herd the day after the ceremony. That wouldn't be happening now. Lots of things weren't going to happen the way they'd been planned. "I really do think you'll pull this off."

"There's no power. There are nearly no guests." She held up her ever-present clipboard. "I like it much better when things go according to plan," she admitted.

"But you're coping like a pro. Adapting, improvising. Seriously, if you manage to make this wedding happen, I guarantee even Samantha will be impressed."

Kelly shook her head. "Rob brought her sandwiches and a flashlight, and the man looked positively smitten with her. Talk about opposites attracting."

"Must be something in the air in Matrimony Valley." He was coming to think of the valley as a special place despite his earlier irritation. Parts of him that felt tied in knots for so long seemed to loosen here, to unfurl out of the grip of grief. As if he were thawing out at the same time the valley was icing over. Was it the town, his time away from the pressures of work, the consuming nature of the wedding-in-crisis…or the friendship of the woman sitting next to him? He couldn't trust that the wedding, the stress and simple lack of sleep weren't messing with his perspective.

"There you are!" An older woman came trotting down the hallway. "I've been looking everywhere for you."

"What now, Rose?" Kelly clearly expected the woman to heap yet another problem onto her shoulders.

"We've solved the problem of the rehearsal dinner—chili in slow cookers. Bill's got a generator and a strip of outlets. Half the town's cooking up a batch, and Yvonne's got ingredients for a s'mores bar. We can make this work."

"A chili and s'mores rehearsal dinner?" Kelly looked skeptical.

Talk about making it up as you go along. "Actually," Bruce found himself saying, "I think it works. Kind of fits in with the rest of the wedding. You don't get any more back-woods than chili and s'mores." Bruce offered Kelly a supportive smile. "I think Darren will approve. And the rehearsal dinner is the responsibility of the groom, isn't it?"

"Well, yes," Kelly said, brightening.

"As best man, I endorse it. So let's go get the groom's approval," Bruce said, rising off the chair.

Chapter Fourteen

At six o'clock that evening, four more guests—including one bridesmaid and one groomsman—had managed to make it into town despite the power still being out. While everyone tried to hold out hopes for improvements tomorrow, optimism was wearing thin. Bruce hoped for everyone's sake that tonight's party would brighten the mood.

He walked downstairs with Carly to an inn lobby that had been totally transformed. "Wow, Daddy!" she gasped.

Bruce had to say he was impressed. How many people could pull off the party atmosphere in a power outage like this? A fire was roaring in the lobby's enormous fireplace, and someone had cleared the local outfitters of every camping lantern it had in stock so that they shone in a rainbow of colors around the room. The whole space had a happy glow about it. The greens he remembered from Kelly's shop were hung around the room with ribbons and strips of plaid flannel.

He didn't know much about how to throw parties, but this place felt more like a party than he'd ever thought possible in a snowstorm. Far smaller than how the event had initially been planned, true, but remarkably cheerful. Happy in spite of it all, which seemed like a particularly potent kind of happiness.

Just outside the inn's front steps, Bruce could see a small army of valley residents manning a collection of grills. Whatever it was they were cooking up, it smelled delicious. On the far side of the room, a battalion of slow cookers simmered hooked up to a power strip whose cord ran out through a window to a running generator outside. He and Carly were among the first downstairs, and Bruce's stomach growled enough from the hard work of the day to make him consider ducking outside to see if he could sneak something right now.

"Daddy, look!" Carly pulled his hand toward where a table had been set up next to the fireplace. "S'mores, just like you said!"

Sure enough, a dessert table of sorts had

been laid out with a cobbled-together collection of s'mores ingredients. Not just the usual chocolate, marshmallows and graham crackers, but surprising things like cherries, nuts, gingersnaps, caramel sauce—and even a few things he couldn't quite identify.

Carly, of course, was ready to try them all. "Can I have one?"

"How about we try dinner first tonight?"

"Aw, why?" She pouted, but only until she spied Lulu coming in from the inn kitchen and the girls raced off to giggle about something together. He didn't have to think twice about letting her run off with her new friend. He knew she'd be safe—that everyone would keep an eye out for her. In his short time here, the town had become a comfortably closed circle, a connected place. As if he'd been living the last two years under glass, and someone was starting to lift the lid. Did every guest snowbound here in the valley feel like that, or was it just him?

He caught sight of Kelly smiling to someone over a wooden bucket filled with greens and red flowers as she placed it on the buffet table. He knew piling everyone into a smaller space helped to keep the temperature comfortable, but it also created an atmosphere he could describe only as "defiant warmth."

It really did feel like the whole valley had pulled together to make this event happen. The inn managed to feel filled with people, even though he knew it was with more "workers" than "guests." The storm had blurred the lines between the two in a surprising and enjoyable way.

Well, mostly enjoyable. Darren was taking the alternative wedding plans a lot better than Tina was. The bride-to-be was still upstairs getting dressed, but Darren had escaped to Bruce's room multiple times in order to decompress and blow off steam from the huge job of keeping Tina happy. "Haven't seen this side of her before," Darren had said nervously as he joined Bruce in the lobby. "Do all wives get like this?"

Sandy had, but not at the wedding. Of course, theirs had gone off without a hitch. Tina and Darren were launching their marriage with a monumental challenge, that was for sure. Bruce clamped a supportive hand on his friend's shoulder. "The way I see it, a lot of marriage is seeing the other person at their worst and loving them anyway. Sandy made for a calm bride, but she was a handful when she was pregnant. You didn't think we went on all those daylong hikes that winter because I liked your company, did you?"

"Ha," Darren said, not laughing.

"Hang in there. You'll be fine and this will be a funny story. Next year, that is."

Darren looked around the room. "I don't know what Tina will do if the power's not back on by tomorrow. Or more guests don't show up."

"Maybe you don't know what to do, but I'm thinking they'll come up with something." Bruce nodded to the setup of chili and corn bread that would join grilled chicken and burgers—and, of course, s'mores—as the rehearsal dinner. As a guy, Bruce found this highly appealing. He could understand, however, that Tina might not share his opinion.

"And then there's her," Darren went on as Rob helped Samantha Douglas into a chair at one corner of the room. "The only thing worse than not getting your perfect wedding is having someone writing about how it all went wrong."

"She wouldn't do that," Bruce replied. "Would she?"

"Tina whined that her Matrimony Valley wedding will never be anything more to *Southeastern Nuptials Magazine* than the place that trapped their reporter and made her limp."

"That's a bit harsh, don't you think?"

"I thought it might be fun for Tina to go ahead with the interview. So we did, and I tried to be nice," Darren offered. "Tina was a little short in the nice department." The groom-to-be sighed. "She's really disappointed, you know? About all the people who called us to say they can't get here. I offered to put it off, but she's always wanted a Valentine's weekend wedding. I was worried for a while that she'd get it in her head to put it off a whole year and try again next February."

Bruce laughed. "I'm with you. That's too long an engagement for any couple." Once he'd decided to marry Sandy, they'd arranged things as fast as possible. He was usually a quick and decisive thinker, which is what made this long slow climb out of grief so excruciating. "You're ready, man. And so is she. Think of it this way—if you can make it through this, you can make it through anything. Just throw a huge Valentine's first anniversary party next year." He handed Darren his flashlight. "As for now, why don't you go get your bride and bring her downstairs so we can get this party started."

As Darren ascended the stairs, Kelly walked up to Bruce with a stunned look on her face.

"What's wrong now?" he asked.

"Funny enough, it's something right." She pushed a stray hair off her forehead.

"That's welcome news. What went right?"

"I just got a compliment from Samantha Douglas."

Bruce looked over at the woman with her bandaged foot carefully placed on an ottoman pillow. "A compliment? From Samantha?"

Kelly grinned. "I know. She said she thought we were handling the situation well. Really well, to be exact."

Samantha had never struck Bruce as the kind of person to be handing out compliments in a good situation, much less this. "Are we sure she didn't hit her head when she fell?"

Kelly laughed. Bruce felt a glow of satisfaction at making the beleaguered florist smile and laugh. It had been a long day for everyone. "I don't know if it's the pain medication or what, but she's been so much nicer since she got hurt. Is that a terrible thing to think?" She stared again at the woman, who was actually smiling as Rob plumped a pillow under her foot. Kelly turned to look at Bruce at the same moment he put the facts together himself. "Could it be…?"

Bruce scratched his chin. "I'm not much of a judge of that sort of thing, but I'd say your hardware store owner is...what'd they call it in *Bambi*? 'Twitterpated'?"

Kelly burst out laughing at that, hand flying to cover her mouth when a few people turned to look. Bruce quickly found something to fiddle with on the table while Kelly pivoted to face the wall. She shot Bruce a sideways glance filled with amusement. "He is, isn't he?"

"You didn't see it yesterday?" he teased. It was fun to one-up her on something so clearly in her territory and not his.

"Well, yes, but..." She sneaked another look at the pair under the guise of adjusting one of the wall sconces. Then she smirked at Bruce. "'*Twitterpated*'? I haven't heard that word in years."

Bruce stuffed his hands in his pockets. "Anyone with a five-year-old daughter going to an elk wedding watches a fair amount of *Bambi*—minus the scary fire scene, of course. Remind me to thank whoever invented the fast-forward button."

Kelly shook her head as she managed another discreet peek at the pair across the room. "Will you look at that?"

At that moment Samantha reached out and touched Rob's hand tenderly. Despite both of their advanced years, they looked as smitten as teenagers. "Who knew your secret weapon was the hardware guy?" he teased.

"Just because Rob strikes her fancy doesn't mean she'll give us a good write-up."

Kelly excelled in finding new things to worry about. "I'd say it certainly can't hurt."

Hailey rang a large brass bell from the bottom of the inn staircase. "Ladies and gentlemen, your bride-and groom-to-be!" With the announcement, the small crowd burst into applause as Darren and Tina came down the stairs and Matrimony Valley's first-ever electricity-free rehearsal dinner kicked into gear.

Just after his second bowl of very good chili, Bruce felt someone tugging on his sleeve. "Mr. Marvin makes chili as good as he makes ice cream, don't you think?" Lulu remarked.

"Is this his recipe?" Bruce asked. "Then I'd have to say I agree."

"I like you." Lulu leaned up against him. "You're fun. And you help Mom have fun. She'd kind of forgot how, if you ask me."

Bruce almost did a double take at the girl's blatant pronouncement. He'd certainly never use the word *fun* to describe himself. "You're pretty fun yourself," he replied, not quite sure what else to say. His nerves sprang to alert as he considered where this odd conversation might be heading—again.

"And Carly. I like her lots. We get along just like sisters, don'cha think?" Lulu crossed her hands over her chest as if that were a harmless observation instead of the relational bombdrop it was.

He tried to give her a serious parental look. They'd already had this conversation once, and he wasn't in a hurry to repeat it. "Friends are always nice to have."

"Sure," Lulu said, "*friends* are nice." She gave the word all the loaded emphasis of someone four times her age.

His double take was less subtle than he would have liked. "You're eight, right?" Eight going on thirty, more like.

She shrugged. "I know what you said, but I see how Mom looks at you. She spent more time on your boutonniere than she did on his." She pointed to Darren. "And he's the groom."

Bruce gave her the "you're making that up" look that usually worked on Carly's tall tales.

"It's true," she defended. "And not just Mom. You should see how fast Miss Hailey said yes when I asked her to sit us all together at the afterward party." Wait, now Kelly and Lulu would be at the wedding reception? When had that happened? *Perhaps when half the invited guests became in danger of not showing up*, he reminded himself.

"The wedding party sits at a head table. And it's the bride who decides who gets to sit where," he argued, feeling like things were spiraling out of his control. Yvonne the baker's insinuations were bad enough, but now they were joined by Hailey the innkeeper?

"I know that," Lulu replied. "That's why I asked Miss Hailey when Miss Tina was right there."

Tina was in on this? Was this a wedding of grown-ups or sixth-grade recess? "I'm sure Carly will be happy to sit next to you at the reception," he said as matter-of-factly as his shock would allow.

She grinned. "That, too."

"But I will be at the head table like the best man ought to be and not sitting with your mother." He pulled her to the nearest couch and had her sit down. "Lulu, this has to stop right now. The valentines were bad enough, but it's starting to get out of hand. I know what you think you see, but your mom and I are not getting together. Not now, and not likely ever. And that doesn't mean you and Carly can't be friends, but it does mean you have to stop what you're doing here."

Her lower lip quivered, and he felt bad about

having to word it so harshly. Only he didn't know how else to squelch this childish effort at "match 'em up" before somebody got hurt.

Against his better judgment, he gave her a hug. "You're a sweet girl, Lulu, and I like you. I'm really glad you and Carly are friends, and I promise we'll come back and visit sometime. But that's all. So go find your mom and enjoy the party, okay?" He regretted putting such a sag in Lulu's shoulders as she crossed the room, but there seemed to be no helping it.

Carly came up to Kelly at the s'mores table with a wide smile. The two girls had been inseparable at the event tonight, and it made Kelly's heart glad to see the friendship becoming so strong. It would be hard when the time came for Carly and Bruce to return to Kinston, but she chose to focus on the present moment. After all, the rehearsal dinner had managed to come off far better than she'd hoped. Maybe she could stand to worry a little less about how everything could go wrong.

"I'm having fun." A telltale smear of chocolate graced the little girl's smile.

"Had a s'more, did you?" Kelly teased, wiping Carly's cheek with a napkin.

"Three." Bruce would have a hard time pulling his daughter down off that sugar high, to be sure. "Daddy said you made Mr. Darren and Miss Tina happy."

Kelly smiled. "Well, I'm very glad to hear that."

"You make Daddy happy, too."

Kelly hoped the rush of warmth she felt in her cheeks didn't show. "That's a nice thing to say, Carly."

"He likes you. Lulu said so, too. We both think that's nice. Do you think it's nice?"

Kelly leaned down to the little girl's height. "Carly, I thought we talked about this already. Your daddy and I are friends, just like you and Lulu are friends." She didn't like how the words had the sour taste of untruth. She did feel a strong pull of attraction to Bruce. Still, now was hardly the time to explain the complexities of adult relationships to a five-year-old. "How about we just concentrate on the wedding right now, sweetie?"

"But I like you. And Lulu. I told Daddy last night I wanted to move here and go to school with Lulu and grow up to run Mr. Marvin's ice-cream shop."

Kelly looked around the room for Bruce, but couldn't find him. "You are always welcome to visit the valley anytime you want. Lulu will always want to play with you while you're here."

"Lulu said the same thing," Carly went on. "She said she'd love to be my big sister."

"Honey, you and Lulu need to stop this. Go find your father and he'll tell you the same thing. This isn't something that can…"

At that moment, the lights flickered on, bringing a cry of relief from everyone in the room. *Thank You, Lord.* Kelly sent a prayer of gratitude heavenward as she leaned back against the wall. "Aren't you glad the lights came back on, Carly?"

She looked down to find Carly gone, back to her father for what she hoped was the final explanation why her ideas about matchmaking were way off course.

"I've never been so grateful to see electric lights in my life!" Hailey exclaimed. "It was going to get frosty in here without power tonight."

"The lights are on," Tina said, hugging Darren. "That must mean the storm is over. Our guests can arrive. We can get married!"

Kelly leaned back against the wall. *We just might make it.* Everyone was hugging each other—guest and valley resident alike—and a chaotic happy celebration filled the room. *Thank You, Lord*, she repeated. *I'm beyond grateful.*

As soon as the commotion died down, Kelly

walked over to where Bruce was plugging the power strip that used to run from the generator outside into a wall outlet inside. "Did you see where they went?"

"Who?" he said as he straightened.

"The girls. I had a conversation with Carly about them matching us up again, and I told her to go find you."

Bruce stood up. "I just had the same talk with Lulu and told her to go find you." He ran a hand down his face. "She didn't take it too well. Lulu's not with you?"

"No. Carly's not with you?"

"No."

The alarm in Bruce's voice hit her like ice water. She spun around and they both scanned the room again. "They're not here." She grabbed Bruce's hand as he looked around with the same growing fear that gripped her throat. "Bruce, they're not here."

Chapter Fifteen

~

"They have to be here," Bruce said. "There isn't anywhere else to be. We just can't see them." He paused for a second before calling out "Carly?"

There was still too much noise in the room to be heard. "Carly!" Bruce called out louder as Kelly called, "Lulu!"

Bill Williams walked by with Ruth. "Everything okay?"

"We can't see the girls," Kelly said with as much calm as she could muster with her heart going off like a fire alarm.

"Oh, they've got to be here," Bill said. "Sneaking into the kitchen for more chocolate, perhaps? Or up to Bruce's room?"

"I left it unlocked," Bruce said, heading for the stairs. Kelly started dashing around the room, asking everyone if they'd seen Lulu or

Carly. No one had—not in the past few minutes anyway.

Bruce came back down the stairs, taking them three at a time. "Not up there."

Panic made the air go thin. "Where could they have gone?"

She tried to think how long it had been since she'd been talking with Carly. Not long, but things had gone a little haywire when the lights came back on. She'd been so caught up in relief that she hadn't paid attention. How could she not pay attention?

Bruce was fighting to stay calm. "It's still nasty outside. They've got to be somewhere in the inn."

Bill stood up on an ottoman near the front of the room. "Does anyone know where Lulu and Carly are?"

One hand clutched at Kelly's chest while the other reached out to Bruce. Heads turned all around the room and murmured questions buzzed through the crowd. She waited for someone to call out, "Here they are!" but no one did.

They wouldn't get the crazy notion to leave the party, would they? She and Bruce had just explained to them—again—that their valentine "wish" wasn't going to happen. Perhaps they were confused and upset enough to want to get away from the celebration.

"Lulu's coat," Kelly said, getting an idea. "Let's go see if it's gone." Together she and Bruce made for the inn's coatroom at a run.

"Not here." Kelly could barely get the words out as she saw the empty hanger next to hers. She turned to Bruce. "Was Carly's gone from your room?"

"I don't know. I didn't think to look. But they have to be together."

"Why on earth would they go outside?"

Bruce stared at her. "To your house. They must have gone to your house."

"That's four blocks from here," Kelly exclaimed. "Why would they go there in this weather?"

"Why do kids do anything?" he barked, grabbing her coat from the hanger and thrusting it at her. "Let's go."

"But your coat…"

He was already heading for the door, grabbing one of the flashlights that Hailey had set out on the lobby table. She ran to keep up with him as he headed straight for his truck parked out front, pulling his keys from his pocket and hitting the fob to unlock the doors. "What are those two thinking?" he said as he gunned the engine and roared out of the parking space, snow flying off the truck as it turned.

"What they've been telling us the whole time—that they want to be together."

He didn't reply but took the corner to her house a bit faster than he should have on the ice. "Slow down, Bruce."

"My five-year-old daughter is out in a snowstorm God knows where and you want me to be patient?" he said as he wrestled the truck back under control. "We should have been watching. We should have been paying attention."

His words lit fire to the panic she was trying to keep in check. She *should* have been paying more attention, keeping an eye on Lulu rather than getting caught up in how the party had wondrously come together. "It's my fault," she said as they reached her house. "I should have been more gentle to Carly when she told me I make you happy."

She regretted not watching her words more carefully, noticing the momentary pause before he shut off the engine. He didn't reply, confirming her suspicion that Lulu had made a similar comment to Bruce. Apparently the girls had planned this. No doubt they were upset it hadn't panned out again. Her heart twisted at the girls' bittersweet, insistent optimism, while her brain ran through a dozen treacherous scenes of snowdrifts, frozen creeks and lost little girls. "Oh, Bruce, what have they done?"

"Hopefully just gone to hide in your house," Bruce said, leaving the truck's headlamps on to illuminate the front yard. "There, look." The wind had whipped the snow, but not so much that she couldn't see the remnants of two recent sets of small footprints leading to the side door where Lulu knew a spare key was hidden under the railing.

"This is my fault," Bruce said as they dashed toward the door, snow gathering on the sweater he wore and in his dark hair. "I should never have…"

"Don't," she said as she pushed open the door, relieved to see it unlocked—further evidence they'd found the girls.

Except they hadn't. The first floor was empty. "Lulu!" she shouted as she ran up the stairs to the dark second floor. Below her she heard Bruce rushing through the house shouting the girls' names. They weren't here. Kelly grabbed at the stair railing, nearly dizzy from panic. The weather could not take someone else she loved. "Father God," she moaned, "don't let them come to harm. Protect them until we find them."

"Where are they?" Bruce yelled into the empty rooms, his eyes lit with fear. "Where'd they go?"

"I don't know," she cried, the mounting panic making it hard to think. "I don't know. This can't be happening."

"It is," he growled, turning in a circle like an angry bear. "C'mon, Kelly, you know Lulu, you know the town. Where would she go? Where would she take Carly to hide?"

How could she answer that? Lulu had never run away, never hidden anywhere except under her blankets, even in the darkest days right after Mark was gone. She strained to make her brain work, to solve this desperate riddle before something terrible happened.

Bruce began hitting every light switch he could find. "Your outside lights—which switch?"

She reached for the switch just as his hand found it, and she wanted to grab that hand and hang on to it. Instead, she pulled away and pointed to the backyard now lit up by the floodlights above the back door. The yard was a swirl of snow and light, but there were no little girls to be seen.

Carly was out there in the snow. Carly was out there in the dark. The only thing keeping him from utter panic was the knowledge that she wasn't alone. She was with Lulu. *Don't You dare take her from me*, his furious soul yelled to heaven. *Don't You dare let her come to harm.* It wasn't the first time he'd lobbed threats at the Almighty, and the last time hadn't done him any good, had it?

"The key!" Kelly was calling out, picking up everything on her kitchen counter in search of something. "The rental cabin key. It's not here."

"What?"

"The rental cabin. Out by where the woodpile is. I was cleaning it out and I had the key on the counter. It's gone."

Bruce ran to the back door and threw it open. "Footprints!" he called back to Kelly as he spied two sets of quickly disappearing tracks trailing toward the cabin behind the garage. He left the door open and yelled, "Carly! Lulu!" into the darkness as he began trudging across the illuminated drifts. "Girls!"

The wind through the branches overhead sent a blast of snow on top of him as he ran, wetting his hair with a cold trickle slipping down the back of his neck. Kelly caught up to him, slipping on the snow.

As he rounded the corner of the garage, three small squares of light glowed through the tangle of bare branches at the end of the property. Sure enough, the line of footprints crossed the clearing, as well. At the sight of the occupied cabin, he grabbed Kelly's hand and began to run. In seconds they'd be hugging the girls in relief, followed by a good scolding for this reckless stunt.

As they reached the far side of the clearing, Bruce sent his flashlight scanning across the structure. "Where's the door?"

"Right there." Kelly pointed, but only to the enormous pile of snow now coating the front of the cabin. "That's where the door is." She let go of his hand and veered off toward the lit window on the side of the cabin.

Bruce looked up at the jagged margin of snow on the roof and worked it out in seconds. Something had jarred the building—maybe one of the girls slamming the door—and the wet and heavy snow must have slid off the roof and piled up against the entrance.

"They're in there!" she yelled to Bruce, who had begun clawing the mound of snow away with his bare hands.

"Mom!" Bruce heard Lulu's muffled voice from inside. His chest filled with relief as he doubled his efforts to scrape the snow away with his stinging bare hands.

"Lulu!" came Kelly's desperate reply. "Are you okay?"

Bruce held it together until he heard the soft cry of "Daddy?" from behind the door. Then he lost it, clawing away the snow with fury.

"Bruce is at the door, girls," he heard Kelly yell. "It's covered in snow and he's digging you out. Just hold on, we'll be right there. I'm going to go help Bruce and we'll be right in."

She came around the side of the cabin. "Where's your shovel?" he called as he kept up the digging. It seemed like a mile of white stood between him and that doorknob. If he could just uncover it, he'd yank that door open no matter how much snow tried to hold it shut.

"It's all the way up by the front door. Here, use these."

She came back with two cedar shingles, tossing one to Bruce. They were cumbersome shovels, but he and Kelly worked side by side to let the planks bite into the drift and uncover most of the door. With a determined growl, Bruce pulled the door open against the last of the snow, sending a narrow wedge of light out into the night. He pushed into the cabin and pulled Kelly in behind him.

They were immediately each hit by a pair of tiny clutching arms and a wave of cries. "I'm sorry, I'm sorry," Lulu kept saying to Kelly, while Carly simply sobbed into Bruce's chest as he lifted her up.

"You're okay, it's okay," he murmured into the top of Carly's hair, holding his daughter so tight it was hard to breathe.

"Thank God you're not hurt," Kelly cried.

Bruce put Carly down and knelt in front of her, holding her shoulders in his red chapped hands. Surely there wasn't anything in any parenting book anywhere covering a moment like this. "Sweetheart, why?"

"Because Miss Kelly said we couldn't stay. You said so, too."

"This is a vacation, Carly. We can't stay here all the time."

"Like the unicorns?"

"Your unicorns?" Bruce asked, thoroughly confused. Wasn't this about him and Kelly? "What did that have to do with what happened tonight?"

"They went away. Today," Carly said in a serious tone.

The unicorns went away now? At the reindeer wedding? How was he supposed to interpret that? "I don't understand, sweetheart." He couldn't fathom what her imaginary unicorns had to do with the crisis they'd just gone through, but her face was so intent. The detail clearly had a great significance to her.

"The unicorns. They said goodbye today."

Bruce's heart twisted in two. Was this Carly giving up? Or growing up? He could barely bring himself to ask, "Mommy's unicorns?" as he smoothed a curl back from her forehead.

Carly shook her head. "They're not Mommy's anymore."

What was he supposed to do with that? He'd never really understood why Carly invented them in the first place, so he was at a loss to understand why she'd chosen—even on an unconscious level—for them to leave. Stumped, Bruce asked, "Are you sad?"

She took a moment to think about it. "No, I'm older than that now."

He caught Kelly's eyes over the top of Carly's head, her smile bringing his own out of hiding. "Okay," he said, not entirely sure what he was agreeing to, save for Carly's apparent sense of closure. It was probably unwise to try to make sense of this now. After all, "this" was sitting in a frozen cabin, in the middle of a snowstorm, having dashed out of the rehearsal dinner of a nearly canceled wedding, discussing the departure of imaginary unicorns.

He looked from Carly to Kelly, and even to Lulu, who gave him a "sounds good to me" shrug.

Kelly said, "I still don't understand why you ran out of the party like this."

"You wouldn't listen to us. You're going to leave after the wedding. I don't want Carly to leave. Carly doesn't want to leave."

"But we haven't even had the wedding yet," Bruce said. The moment the words were out, he realized the girls weren't thinking in terms of logic. They were just unhappy little girls who wanted to be together. It didn't occur to them that running away tonight would do absolutely nothing to fix their problems. They just knew they were sad that their wishes weren't coming true.

"I don't wanna go home," Carly said, sniffling. "I wanna stay here."

"Mom, I don't think you want Carly's dad to leave after the wedding, either. You've been so happy."

"Happy?" Kelly questioned, sitting on the nearest chair. "Lulu, honey, this is the worst week I've had in years. I've been absolutely frantic."

Lulu shrugged. "Maybe, but like I told Mr. Bruce, you've been anyway. Happy, I mean. You make each other happy, and Carly and I like that. A lot."

"What I like is knowing my little girl is

safe," Kelly said as she pulled Lulu onto her lap. "I was really scared. We both were."

"Why can't we stay, Daddy? I like it here. You don't get far away anymore."

Bruce sighed. "It's not as simple as all that. But I really have enjoyed our visit and I'm sure we can come back."

Kelly tried to save him. "Everyone back at the party is very worried about you. People stopped everything to help us look for you. Don't you think we should head back or at least call the inn?"

"You hugged her. You said you thought she was pretty," Carly said with a frustrating persistence.

Kelly turned pink, and not from the cold. There didn't seem much point in denying. "Well, yes, I did say that Lulu's mother is pretty."

"I don't get it," Lulu said, sliding off her mother's lap. "You like him. He likes you. Carly and I like each other. This is Matrimony Valley, for crying out loud."

"Lulu!" Kelly gasped.

"Well, it is. Everybody else gets married here, why can't you?"

Kelly threw up her hands. "Don't you think this is a discussion for another time?"

"Not really," Lulu replied as Carly shook her head.

"May I remind you that Bruce and I just traipsed out here worried sick with fear without hats or gloves and after putting a damper on Tina and Darren's rehearsal dinner?"

Bruce wanted to sit down and sink his head into his hands, but instead he gathered up Carly's coat. "We're done here, girls. Gather your things."

"Dad…"

"I was gonna hang our red heart in our window and everything if you said yes," Lulu pouted to her mother.

"Lulu told me," Carly said, "whenever anyone…"

"Let's just get back to the inn and let everyone know you're okay." He hadn't even had a chance to call back there and let Darren, Tina and the others knew they'd found the girls, so he pulled his phone from his jacket pocket and texted a quick All's well. Exhaustion surged as the adrenaline of his fear faded away, and Kelly looked like she was running on empty, as well. Neither one of them had had a decent night's sleep in days, and tomorrow was the wedding.

He looked at Carly as he finished zipping

up her jacket. "Running away like this didn't solve anything did it?"

"Not really. It was scary."

"You two are going to have to let Bruce and me work this out by ourselves," Kelly said, catching Bruce's eyes over her daughter's head. Her cheeks were flushed and snow had wet her hair as tears wet her eyelashes. *She is pretty. She's beautiful.* The thought came to him without any warning and refused to go away. *Smart and pushy and stubborn and beautiful.* It stunned him to realize he'd been digging through that mound of snow for her and Lulu as much as for Carly. There was a part of him that wanted to stay as much as Carly did.

"Daddy, where's your coat?" Carly asked. "Don't you know to wear a coat when it's cold outside?"

He started to give her a long explanation of how daddies don't think about cold and coats when they're frightened for their precious little girls, but instead he just held her to his chest and managed to laugh.

Chapter Sixteen

The morning of the wedding dawned with the bright blue of a storm-swept sky. With the girls safe and sound and the power back on, everything seemed a brilliant white. Even the lingering frosting of ice, despite having caused so much trouble yesterday, seemed to coat everything with a crystalline beauty. If you ignored all the people who couldn't get here, thought Bruce as he looked out the window, it'd be a perfect day for a winter wedding.

He gazed around the quiet town. So many people had pulled together to make Tina and Darren's rehearsal dinner a happy occasion last night. It felt as if every person in the valley had pitched in. Lots had gone wrong leading up to today's ceremony, but the spunk of this tiny valley led him to believe that a lot would go surprisingly right. Power outages, airport shutdowns, spontaneous potluck rehearsal dinners, runaway girls, one very complex and fascinating florist—this wedding has always been "unusual," but right now he'd classify it as "unforgettable."

A little pair of flannel pajama'd arms flung around his legs. "G'morning, Daddy," Carly said with a wide yawn.

"Good morning, sunshine."

"Did everybody get here?" She evidently thought the return of the power would solve all the wedding's logistical problems.

"No," he said. "But it's sunny out, so maybe a few more will be able to make it in before the ceremony starts."

"What if they don't?"

"Well, do you remember what Miss Kelly said we needed for a wedding?"

She held up her outstretched fingers. "Bride, groom, minster—" her mispronunciation made him smile "—and God."

"Do we have those four things?" It felt foolish—and then again, perhaps very wise—to ask a five-year-old if God was present. He was just coming to grips with what a huge detour his faith had taken in the past two years, where it seemed like Carly's never wavered at all.

She grinned. "Yep."

"Well, then," he said, tickling her under her chin until she flopped on the bed in a pile of giggles, "sounds to me like we're all set. Except—" he flopped down beside her "—if you ask me, an extra-special flower girl is absolutely necessary."

"And we've got that!"

"But our flower girl needs a good breakfast. If they've got power downstairs, that must mean waffles." After last night's fiasco and all that had led up to it, Bruce had been so sure today would feel heavy. He was certain the huge void of Sandy's absence would weigh him down, and steal his joy.

Instead, an inexplicable lightness filled him. As if he really could be just plain…happy today. *Thank You.* The small, silent prayer required no effort at all. Despite all that had happened, the idea that God had cleared the way for Tina and Darren didn't seem such an impossible thought to hold. And that maybe, somewhere not too far off in the future, God would make a clearer way for him.

"Are you nervous about today?"

She thought about it for a second. "Not really. I think Miss Kelly will make everything work out."

Kelly was likely a bundle of nerves today.

Despite pulling off nothing short of a wonder with last night's party, she was probably already hard at work to make Tina and Darren's wedding day as perfect as possible. They'd not had any chance to talk about everything that had happened last night, and Kelly had been on his mind constantly.

Rather than be uncomfortable, Bruce found himself a bit, well, *twitterpated* with how she occupied his thoughts. As if her pushy invasiveness had somehow transformed to a companionship he couldn't quite resist. *What am I supposed to do with that?* He was surprised to discover he couldn't tell if the notion was a thought or a prayer.

"You went away again, Daddy."

"Did I?"

"Only you didn't frown this time."

He looked at her. "Do I frown when I go away?"

"You did before," she said.

He took this opportunity to ask something that had been on his mind as much as Kelly since last night. "Carly, honey, can you explain to me again why the unicorns went away?"

"'Cuz they're done, like I said."

"Done with what?"

"Us. They have to go to other little girls and daddies now."

He still didn't really understand, but he wanted to. "What do other little girls and daddies need from them that we don't anymore?"

"To know their mommies are in heaven. Mommy sent the unicorns to watch us." She kept looking at him like he should understand.

"So we don't need watching anymore?"

"Uh-huh."

"Why not?" It seemed that she'd decided they had turned a corner somehow, and while he felt the same lightening of spirit, he wanted to know how she'd describe it.

"'Cuz." Finding that answer sufficient, she grabbed her stomach. "Daddy, I'm hungry."

That was all the insight he was going to get, at least for now. Whatever emotional reassurance Carly's unicorns had provided, the need had been met and she'd moved on. He was sure Pastor Mitchell might have something to say about it, or Carly's counselor, but the settled nature of his heart really was sufficient for now. "I'm hungry, too. Let's go get some breakfast—it's gonna be a big day."

They dressed quickly and came down the stairs to a dining room loud with chatter from all members of the elk wedding party. Not only had the arrival of power lifted everyone's spirits, but also he noticed a few new guests had made it in.

"There's our flower girl!" Darren called from behind a groom-worthy stack of waffles. "And the best man," he added when Bruce gave him a "don't I count?" look. "Join me for waffles, Carly-girl."

"How's the bride?" Bruce asked as he and Carly took seats at Darren's table. "Any calmer?"

"Well, getting there," Darren answered. "Power helps. I gotta admit, I didn't want to get near that woman if she didn't have a working blow-dryer or curling iron today."

"You're not supposed to see her before the wedding anyway," Bruce advised.

"She'll be extra pretty," Carly said.

"So will you," Darren said, gently poking Carly's nose.

"I know. Miss Kelly's made me a special headband and everything."

"You and Miss Kelly seem to get along really well." Darren addressed his reply to Bruce rather than to Carly.

"The girls like each other," Bruce answered.

Darren smirked. "That, too."

Bruce went to shoot Darren a dark look, but found he couldn't.

* * *

Kelly was on her third cup of coffee when the phone rang.

"I'm just calling to tell you you're ready for today," Jean's voice came over the line.

"I don't feel ready," she replied. "There are a million things that aren't done. That might not get done."

"Kelly Nelson," Jean said, "you are better at plan B than anyone else in the valley. I heard nothing but great things about last night's rehearsal dinner."

"Including the crisis with Lulu and Carly?" Kelly looked up the staircase where her daughter still slept. "She's never pulled something like that. Of all the nights…"

"More of the valentine nonsense?" Jean asked, adding, "That isn't really nonsense?"

Nothing was ever really private in a town this size. Not with friends like Jean and Yvonne, at least. "The girls have got it in their heads that Bruce and I belong together."

"Are they wrong?"

Kelly sat down at one of the kitchen counter stools. "I could give you a dozen reasons why they're wrong." Even she could hear how unconvinced her voice sounded.

"Maybe those reasons don't matter as much as the reasons why they're right."

Kelly didn't reply. Her heart had been discounting every sensible reason Bruce was a bad idea since he'd held her in the hardware store.

"You've been alone long enough, Kelly," Jean went on. "And you're great at it—you're resourceful and independent and all kinds of things like that. I'd be sunk without you, and this weekend so would half the valley. None of that will go away if you let Bruce into your life, you know."

"And Lulu's," Kelly cautioned. "Come on, Jean, you've been a single mom. You know the stakes go way up on things like this when a child's involved. Bruce lives in Kinston, on the other side of the state. And he's a pilot. I don't think I can do that again."

"The other end of North Carolina isn't the other end of the world. And I think you could do anything. Even have another pilot in your life. Are you really going to let what happened to Mark stop you from trying with someone who could be incredibly good for you and Lulu?"

"But does it have to be now? On top of everything?" The list on her clipboard didn't leave much room for breathing, much less pondering risky relationships.

"Maybe it has to be now *because* of everything. It's all going to be fine, Kelly. We'll pull off the elk wedding of the year and *Nuptials* will write up a rave review."

Kelly let her head fall into her hands. "Samantha? I have no idea what she's going to say about this weekend."

"Stop worrying. She's going to think it's amazing."

"Hey," Kelly said to her friend, "I'm the one who usually gives you a boost. Who pulled the switcheroo?"

Jean laughed. "I'm an old married woman now, remember?"

"You can't be old. If you're old, then I'm older." In truth, Kelly had only a little over a year on her friend, even if she was the more experienced parent. And even though Jean had seen her own share of hardships as a parent, Kelly had always felt that her widow status made her feel a whole decade older than her friend. Thirty-one was still young, but there were days lately when Kelly felt the years press down hard. Maybe that's why the weariness in Bruce's eyes had called to her so. And why the light returning to them was in real danger of stealing her heart.

"You're doing great," Jean encouraged. "Really. We'd all be sunk without the way you took the lead on this. I fully intend to be sitting in a pew to watch Darren and Tina tie the knot this afternoon. In a wedding nature tried very hard to cancel, but is happening because my favorite stubborn, brilliant florist found a way. So find a way in this. God may surprise you."

Kelly looked up at the clear sky, remembering the storm they'd just weathered. "I've had more than enough surprises for one wedding. But I do see your point. In all of it." After a pause, she added, "I'm…well, I'm scared."

"I know," Jean said softly. "But you're also the bravest person I know. And I love you and I want you to be happy. Well, happi*er*, because I know you were about to say 'I'm happy now.' Or have you forgotten a previous version of this conversation where you convinced me to let Josh back into my life? It turned out pretty good, remember?"

Kelly felt herself smile. "Brilliantly."

"There you have it. See you at the wedding," Jean said.

Kelly ended the call and pointed her finger at the clipboard. "You hear that? Brilliance. Time to make the most brilliant improvised snowbound wedding Matrimony Valley and *Southeastern Nuptials Magazine* has ever seen."

Chapter Seventeen

Kelly settled the last arrangement on the altar. They were going to make it. Sure, it wasn't perfect—buckets of things had gone wrong with this wedding—but she'd managed to make it special, and that's what mattered. *Thank You, Jesus*, she praised as she leaned against the front pew and surveyed her creations. *I feel like I need to sleep for a week, but we made it.*

She heard the church doors open behind her, and turned to see Bruce walking in. She hadn't seen him all day, nor had she ever seen him dressed in anything other than casual clothes. While the backwoods style of the wedding placed him in only a plaid shirt and gray flannel vest, he looked extraordinarily handsome.

And satisfyingly impressed with her decorations. His expression made her chest glow with pride at how beautiful the church looked despite not having half the flowers she and Tina had planned.

"I wish everyone could be here to see what you've done with the place," Bruce said as he walked up the aisle. "I hope Tina doesn't feel like the place is half-empty." Only about a third of the invited guests had managed to arrive.

"Oh, but that's the best part," she replied, walking to meet him. "It won't be."

"What do you mean?"

"Mayor Jean wrote a few emails and sent her husband out on a few recruiting calls this afternoon. The entire town has promised to show up and fill the sanctuary for today's ceremony."

His wide smile only made him more handsome. "That's pretty amazing."

It was easy to smile back. "Matrimony Valley's a pretty amazing place."

"Speaking of amazing, I don't know if you noticed in all the chaos of last night, but when I got back to the hotel I saw Samantha Douglas getting a very sweet good-night kiss from Rob."

"Oh, my," she replied. "If Samantha gives us a good write-up after everything that's happened, I'll tell Rob he can have free flowers for the rest of the year."

Bruce laughed. "If you ask me, he'll be sending some to a certain wedding writer on a regular basis."

She grinned. "I can make that happen."

They stood, side by side, in the quiet of the church for a moment. This day was loaded for him in ways that had nothing to do with what was transpiring between the two of them. There were a million things she wanted to say, to ask, but she settled on softly asking, "How are you doing?"

When he pulled in a deep breath, Kelly steeled herself for a sad reply. "You know, it's not so bad. I'm happy for Darren." He looked at her for a long moment, and Kelly felt her stomach flip. "Actually, I'm sort of happy, period." He rubbed the back of his neck. "Not quite sure how that happened."

The way he looked told her he knew, as did she, exactly how that had happened. That, in spite of everything, the space between them had filled with an unexpected potency. Even last night's drama couldn't take away how here, alone with him amid all these creations she'd worked so hard to make, in a place so near and dear to her heart, Bruce felt…close.

Against her wishes, the lines between Matrimony Valley's promise of a happy ending and her own belief in something like that for herself were blurring. Of course, it was easy to embrace hope today, inside the emotional bubble of Tina and Darren's wedding. Tomorrow or someday very soon, that bubble would pop.

"Did you get Carly's hair sorted out?" Kelly asked, needing to fill the silence.

"Yeah. The girls are up in the bridal suite getting all glammed up. The headband ought to work great, Tina tells me. Thanks for that."

"She'll be adorable. I'll make sure Lulu makes a fuss over how perfect she looks, but I don't think I'll have to say much to persuade her. Lulu's so excited to get to come to the wedding anyway."

He leaned against the pew opposite her, so that they stood on either side of the aisle. Their voices echoed in the empty sanctuary, but still the place felt close and intimate. "That's a great idea," he said in a fumbling tone. "Filling the church for them and all."

They were both talking about inconsequential things, making noise so they didn't talk about the very consequential thing happening between them. The fluster Kelly felt belonged to a teenager, not a woman of her years, not a professional working hard to make an event go off smoothly. Still, his praise, his gratitude for the effort being made here, warmed her.

"I hope Samantha goes on for pages about how well you all did. She ought to give Matrimony Valley a five-star rave, or whatever a great write-up is called."

"Yes," she agreed. "I'm starting to believe we really are going to get a happy ending here. Unconventional, but happy."

"That's what matters, isn't it?"

Another stretch of silence fell between them. "Do you think…?" He started, then stalled, fussing with the burlap loop of one of the pew decorations. "Do we get a second one? People like us, that is?"

She knew what he meant, but she asked anyway. "A second what?"

"Happy ending, I guess. Or do we just… learn how to be happy for…other people's happiness." He seemed to lose his nerve just then, turning as if he might leave, then turning back again. "Maybe it's just the valley. The whole happily-ever-after of the place. I…" The word hung in the air, an unfinished sentence.

It wasn't the valley. Or at least it wasn't *all* the valley. Nor the wedding—although she knew that the wedding atmosphere amplified it in a way. Even far away from here or other weddings, however, Kelly knew she would feel this pull between them. She enjoyed the way he made her laugh. She both admired and was annoyed by Bruce's indulgent splurges like ice cream before dinner and hopscotch on a hotel room carpet. Things like that seemed to take so much effort for her anymore.

And then there was how he looked at her—as if she were a beacon, as if her company was a gift to him. It satisfied some need she'd denied since Mark was gone: to be the person who made someone else better, stronger, more alive.

"Well," she began, feeling her cheeks warm with heat, "I think we get to *want* happy endings. Everybody wants happy endings."

"Thanks to you, Darren and Tina are getting their crack at happiness despite everything. Only…"

"Only what?"

"Don't you want Lulu to believe there's all the happiness she needs in the world? Life's taken a lot from her and Carly. Don't you think they should grow up feeling like all kinds of joy is possible for them?"

That is exactly what she believed. "Maybe that's why I was so quick to get behind the idea of Matrimony Valley—because it shows Lulu all the possibilities that I…well…" She couldn't finish the thought. Not safely, at least.

Suddenly she was tired enough to disregard all the reasons why talking about love and happiness with Bruce Lohan was unwise. The thought of resting for a few moments of peaceful quiet in a back pew with her head against Bruce's broad shoulder was entirely too strong a lure, not to mention unlikely if not impossible.

"Well," she said, straightening her shoulders, "I've got a wedding to stage and you've got one to be in." She checked her watch. "See you in a little over an hour." She began to gather up her tools.

He put a hand on her arm to stop her. She felt every finger, every inch of his palm against her sleeve. "Kelly," he said.

She stopped, fighting the urge to close her eyes. She didn't respond because she didn't trust her voice to betray how shaky and vulnerable she felt.

"It'll be amazing, you know. This wedding. You'll have pulled it off despite everything. I'm glad for that, and not just because Tina and Darren are my friends."

The admiration in his voice sank to some deep, formerly hollow place that suddenly felt filled. At least halfway filled. She needed to leave now before she did something truly foolish like look up into his eyes.

Instead, she grabbed for her bag of tools and tucked all the remaining ribbon inside as fast as she could. "I'm glad for that, too," she said, and deliberately slowed her steps toward the little back room behind the altar.

Slowed, because her heart was telling her to run.

Fifteen minutes later, Lulu's eyes popped wide and her mouth hung open in a stunned "oh" as Jean, Josh and Jonah brought her into the sanctuary.

"It's amazing," Jean admired.

"Half the flowers weren't the ones Tina wanted, I had to mix two different reds with the ribbons and add in burlap, and the candles are a mix of what I had in the shop because the order didn't come in."

"It's still amazing," Jean repeated.

"Two-thirds of the wedding guests won't be here. The groom's own parents aren't going to make it, nor will the ring bearer."

Jean grabbed her hand. "And it's *still* amazing."

"This stressed-out florist is dangling by her last perfectionist nerve, Jean."

"Nevertheless, very soon Mr. and Mrs. Darren Billings are going to become Matrimony Valley's next husband and wife."

"And probably our most memorable wedding," Kelly added.

"So far," Jean added with a wink.

"Let's go sit you down," Josh said to his wife. "Somebody is supposed to still be resting her ankle." He gave the words a teasing emphasis, knowing she needed to be off her feet for happier reasons.

The door opened, letting in a whoosh of the still-frigid air as Rob Folston helped a beautifully dressed Samantha through the door to settle delicately on one of the back pews.

"Look what you've done with the place," Samantha said. A joke, an actual smiling joke from Samantha Douglas. "How'd you pull it off?"

"It's what we do," Kelly replied.

"It's what Mama does best," boasted Lulu with a pride that warmed Kelly's heart.

"You're rather early," Kelly commented. "I hope everything is okay?"

"Robert though it would be best if I didn't have to jostle in with the rest of the guests," Samantha said.

No one in the valley called Rob Folston "Robert." Then again, no one in the valley had seen him in the suit coat and tie he currently wore. Kelly hid her smile at the too-transparent smitten nature of the kindly store owner. "Falling" for someone would never mean the same thing in her eyes after this unlikely match.

"And I wanted to talk to you," Samantha went on. "We've not had a chance to really chat, you and I. Can you spare some time now, or do you have last-minute things to attend to?"

"No," answered Kelly. "I'm actually ready. Or as ready as I'll ever be. All we need now is…"

Lulu popped up beside her. "A bride, a groom, a minister and God."

"Oh, I think it takes a bit more than that, dear," said Samantha.

"Not according to Mom," Lulu countered.

"Lulu," said Kelly, "why don't you pick out where we'll sit for the ceremony."

Lulu looked surprised. "Next to Carly and Mr. Lohan, of course."

"Oh, no, we can't. They're part of the wedding party. They need to sit up front. We're just guests, so we'll need to sit farther back." When Lulu looked disappointed, Kelly shooed her off with a "we'll talk about this later" look.

"She's darling," Samantha said.

"She can be a handful, but she is darling. Thank you."

"If you're looking for someone to thank

then you should make sure you take a moment to thank that best man."

Kelly sat sideways in the pew just in front of Samantha and turned so they faced each other. "Why is that?"

"He just caught Robert and me in the lobby of the inn and gave a big speech about how impressed and complimentary I should be of Matrimony Valley and the job it's done."

She was still hearing praises from Samantha as Bruce and Darren appeared, laughing between themselves as if nothing at all had gone wrong in this all-gone-wrong wedding. When Bruce sent a smile her direction, her breath caught in a way that had nothing to do with professional anxiety.

She'd chosen a swirly forest green dress with a plaid wool shawl and boots for the occasion. Professional, practical, but with a touch of style while still in keeping with the wedding's themes. As she finished with Samantha and brought the box of boutonnieres over to the groomsmen, she caught Bruce staring and felt her cheeks flush.

"And here's the man of the hour," she said to Darren as she handed him his boutonniere. "You look wonderful. Ruggedly handsome."

The groom grinned down at the tuft of red, burlap and greenery as she pinned it to his vest. "Not bad, Lohan. Tina put her faith in the right place."

Bruce laughed. "That place would be with Kelly. I didn't have a whole lot to do with these except to say 'okay.'"

"A wise man always knows a good idea when he sees it," Kelly said. She hesitated just a moment as she held up Bruce's boutonniere. "Now hold still."

It was a perfectly ordinary thing for a florist to pin on a groomsman's boutonniere. Still, the task felt intimate, almost flirtatious. A long-lost effervescence filled her as she slid her hand under his vest to fix the pin. The warmth of his chest seemed to radiate through his shirt, and she wondered if the faster heartbeat she felt under her hand was all in her imagination.

"We got three of the four," Bruce said a bit too softly, nodding to Pastor Mitchell, who was fiddling with something at the pulpit. "And the bride is on her way."

Hailey was tasked with the transport of Tina, her parents and the two bridesmaids who had made it in before the storm. Kelly would meet them in the choir room to fuss with bouquets and any last-minute arrangements. "How is she?" Kelly asked.

"Way better than this time yesterday," Darren cut in, straightening his bow tie for the fifth time. "How much fun everyone had at the blackout rehearsal dinner helped to calm her down."

Suddenly everything had a title. The Elk Wedding—or Reindeer Wedding, depending on the age of the person you asked—now was also the Snowbound Wedding, preceded by the Blackout Rehearsal Dinner and, if God was kind, the Very Nice but Very Small Reception. There was even a slim chance a few more of the guests would arrive in time to catch the reception. This really was going to go down as the craziest wedding in Matrimony Valley history.

"Doesn't Daddy look nice?" Carly came up, looking absolutely adorable in a ruffled red flannel dress, bright red tights and the little brown hiking boots with red lace laces. The little girl tossed her head with glee, clearly loving the curls Matrimony Valley's stylist had given her. And yes, the headband added just the right touch.

"Yes, your father looks very nice," Kelly replied, keeping her eyes on Carly for fear of revealing how truly handsome she found Bruce. "And you look extra pretty yourself."

Carly executed an extravagant twirl, reveling in how the full ruffled skirt billowed up. "I look just like a reindeer princess." She wagged her fingers at Darren, calling him down to her level, where she whispered, "Wait until you see Miss Tina. She looks extra-extra pretty."

Darren smiled. "She always looks extra-extra pretty to me."

Bruce gave a laugh. "This guy's got what it takes to be married, if you ask me."

Kelly checked her watch. "Nearly there. Carly, you come back with me to where the ladies are. Bruce, go make sure your groom is back behind the sanctuary and come out when Pastor gives you the signal." She gave Darren a warm smile and grabbed his arm. "You made it. You're getting married. It's finally happening."

Safely hidden behind the altar, Bruce watched Darren adjust his bow tie yet again. They were alone—the second groomsman was filling in as an usher and would join them at the last minute before the procession started. "If I didn't know any better, I'd say this thing was shrinking," Darren gulped.

Bruce put a hand on his friend's shoulder. "The pastor who married Sandy and me told me if a man doesn't shake in his shoes the day he gets married, he doesn't fully understand what he's about to do."

"I've got that covered," Darren said. He looked at Bruce with stunned eyes. "I'm getting married."

Bruce laughed. "Despite everything. I gotta tell you, man, *being* married is going to be so much easier for you than *getting* married was. This'll be a great story…someday. I'm happy for you." He truly was. A part of him worried that he wouldn't honestly be able to say that today, that the press of his own grief wouldn't allow for joy, but it wasn't that way. He felt Sandy's memory as a distant hum, but not a deafening roar.

Bruce peeked through the small glass window into the sanctuary again, watching Kelly. She looked beautiful in a deep green knit dress that made her eyes shine even from this distance. It was feminine, but sensible and cozy—suiting her personality perfectly. He couldn't stop himself from singing her praises to Samantha Douglas when they'd bumped into each other in the inn half an hour ago. Who would have thought he'd become such a big fan of Matrimony Valley?

"You're staring," came Darren's voice next to him.

"No, I'm not."

Darren bumped his shoulder playfully. "Yeah, you are. Glad to see it. You've been smiling, too, and that's been gone for a while." The groom leaned against the wall. "Is it hard? Today? Without her? If I feel the hole she left, it must be a canyon for you."

Bruce leaned beside him, grateful for his friend's honesty. "I was worried it'd be bad. The loss is there—it's always there—but better than I thought."

"You know," Darren said, stuffing his hands in his pockets, "if Tina and I have half the marriage you and Sandy had, I'll be grateful. You guys were amazing. All the way through everything."

"It helps to have an amazing woman, and you've got one of those. You and Tina, you'll be great together. You already are."

Darren nodded toward the window looking into the sanctuary. "Amazing's not a one-shot deal, you know. I think amazing can happen twice. Certain things about this town strike me as pretty amazing."

"Enough with the amazing." Bruce shot Darren a look. "Today's about you and Tina."

Darren grinned. "I'd be okay sharing, you know. Enough happiness to go around and all that."

"I wouldn't say that in front of your bride," Bruce teased. "Even with everything that's gone haywire, this is still her day."

"Oh, I get that," Darren replied. "But you should also know that Tina went out of her way to make sure Hailey sat you and Kelly together at the reception. Well, Lulu and Carly, too, but somehow I don't think this was about little girls." He grabbed Bruce's arm. "It'd be great to see you happy again. Don't miss a chance when it's right in front of you."

"Let's just get you married before something else goes wrong," Bruce said, brushing off the warmth Darren's comments kindled in his chest. "I think that's enough of an agenda for a day like today."

Chapter Eighteen

Kelly lined up each of the two bridesmaids ahead of the bride, placing Carly just in front of the entry door she'd open in a few minutes. The sounds of the church organ filled the building, and Kelly sent up a prayer of thanksgiving that the power had been restored. Last night she'd feared she'd have to ask Marvin to bring his accordion.

"Miss Tina looks beautiful, doesn't she?" Carly said.

"She does. And so do you." Carly did look adorable.

"I love my headband." The child posed like a princess with her birch wood basket of flower petals.

"That makes me happy." Kelly glanced down the entranceway to ensure that the two bridesmaids were ready in line. Bruce and the maid of honor had been given the rings to hold since the ring bearer ended up stuck in Indianapolis. Everything was as ready as it would ever be.

"You look beautiful, too," Carly added.

Kelly hoped the rush of warmth she felt in her cheeks didn't show. "That's a nice thing to say, Carly."

"Has Daddy told you he likes you? I know he does. Lots."

Kelly leaned down to Carly's height. "How about we concentrate on the wedding right now, sweetie?" She pointed to the basket. "Get some in your hand. We're going to start." Kelly pulled open the door that led into the sanctuary, and sent the final groomsman to his post beside Bruce and Darren. She pointed down the aisle. "There's your daddy, and you drop these petals along the aisle as you walk toward him nice and slow just like you practiced. Are you ready?"

Carly held up a tiny handful of red petals. "Yep."

Kelly looked over to the side of the sanctuary where Samantha's photographer was stationed. The man had kindly offered to use his equipment to record and live-stream the ceremony to Darren's parents still stranded in Ohio. Really, there wasn't a single person in the valley today who hadn't pitched in in some way to make this wedding happen—even the out-of-towners like the photographer. Today of all days, this town earned its name of Matrimony Valley.

The processional music began. Carly's adorably nervous smile led Kelly to give the girl a kiss on the top of her head as she waved her on her way. There was no denying how fond she had grown of Carly. Lulu had made some casual friendships with valley children before, but the near-instant and sister-like bond she'd made with Bruce's daughter truly seemed rare and special.

Carly made her way down the aisle, earning coos and whispers of "Isn't she adorable?" from the valley residents and wedding guests who had gathered to fill the church. The only person who wasn't here was Yvonne, because she was back in her shop. She'd launched into a furious surge of baking once the power came back on in order to have a wedding cake ready by the time the reception started.

When Carly was halfway to Bruce, Kelly sent the first bridesmaid down the aisle. The second followed, and then the all-important pause as the congregation stood and the organist began the "Bridal Chorus."

For all the stress and strain, for all the compromises and makeshift preparations, Tina looked glorious and glowing with happiness as she stepped into the doorway. As Mayor Jean had advised, Kelly held a gentle hand out to Tina's father to ensure that Tina paused, then looked at the top of the aisle to see Darren's face transform at the sight of his bride.

Jean always said that moment was the fuel that kept her going, and Kelly could see why. It was nothing short of wonder, a little piece of everything that was still right in the world. A pure moment of love's power to conquer all.

She tried not to let her gaze wander to Bruce as she touched Tina's father's elbow as a signal to begin. Still, it was as if she couldn't help but catch Bruce's eyes as the bride went to meet her groom. This day had become such a mix of emotions between them; work and joy, fear and accomplishment, remembered love and endured loss. She saw it all in his expression, just as she was sure he could see it in hers.

What they were feeling was true, wasn't it? Not just a product of today and all the chaos that had led up to it? It felt true—powerfully true—but so did all the reasons why it ought to be impossible. She was too tired to trust how his gaze sent her pulse dancing. Too swept up in the moment to believe how his compliments and admiration felt as if it made her skin glow.

She was tearing up because she always teared up at weddings. Not because some defiant part of her had started to believe another happy ending might be possible for her. That disobedient hope had slipped out of her control, unstoppable as the water down Matrimony Falls.

"Dearly beloved," Pastor Mitchell began, "we are gathered here to celebrate the victory of love over just about every hurdle we can imagine."

While everyone laughed, Kelly was surprised to see the bridesmaids and groomsmen break into jubilant applause. Applause? Now? Congregants often applauded when the bride and groom were announced as man and wife at the end of the ceremony, but then again, didn't Tina and Darren deserve congratulations for simply making it to this moment, as well? She felt new tears slip down her cheeks as she joined in the cheerful display. It was unconventional, but what about this wedding had ever been conventional?

"Now," said Pastor Mitchell, raising his hands to quiet the ovation, "shall we get down to business?" And with that, he began the happy, long-awaited task of joining Darren and Tina as man and wife before God, some of their friends and family and nearly all of Matrimony Valley.

Bruce felt someone tug on his sleeve while he waited for Carly to finish up her photographs with the bride and bridesmaids. He turned to find that Lulu had seated herself on the pew next to him.

"It was bee-u-tiful, wasn't it?" she asked, stringing the word out with little-girl glee.

He knew valley residents had filled the pews out of kindness to the newlyweds, but he couldn't deny how right it felt to have Kelly and Lulu in the church to watch the ceremony. He'd told himself it was because of the huge part they'd played in making the wedding happen, but it was more than that. Too much more than just professional investment. He simply couldn't bring himself to squelch the warm glow that filled him when they were around. Kelly most certainly, but Lulu, too. "It sure was beautiful," he answered.

"I really like weddings," Lulu said, swinging her legs. With a smile, Bruce noticed that she'd swapped out her own bootlaces for strips of sparkly purple fabric so that her footwear mimicked Carly's. Lulu's spunk amused him in so many ways.

"That's good, figuring what your mom does and where you live." He sat back, relief mixing with fatigue. He could count the number of hours he'd slept this weekend on one hand—that had to be part of the reason for all this new emotionality messing with his composure. "Once word gets out about how the valley pulled this one off, I expect you'll be one busy town."

"Do you like weddings?"

No. Or I didn't. More scared of them, maybe, until today. "Oh, they're fine enough," he replied. "I'm happy for Darren and Tina." It was true. Last week he wasn't sure he could get through the ceremony without feeling like a numb imposter on the fringes of someone else's happiness. Then Kelly caught his gaze across the sanctuary as the wedding started.

Those eyes. That slightly nervous hint of a smile. The tender way she bent down and kissed the top of Carly's head. How on earth does a man get taken in by the curve of a woman's cheek from clear across a big room like that?

For a few seconds, he almost forgot where he was, or how to breathe, or that he used to be numb. Or even that anyone else was in the room. Something inside him that had started to crack open shoveling his way into that cabin last night split wide open today. Something he wasn't sure would—or should—come to life ever again. An uneasy sense of impending— what? Doom? Happiness? Change?—raced up from behind him like a storm he had to outrun to stay on course. He'd had the sense of something changing all weekend, and during today's ceremony he'd realized what it was: the return to living in a world where happiness was once again a possibility.

"I'm glad we get to come to the party," Lulu went on, leaning up against him as if they'd been friends for years. "It's gonna be fun. It's great that Mom and I get to sit with you and Carly."

So the matchmaking was still going full force. He'd been meaning to put a stop to that little scheme to have them sit together, but never got around to it. And it wasn't hard to work out why. The idea of sitting with Kelly at the lantern-lit dinner he knew Tina and Darren had planned felt as tempting as Marvin's sundaes. To watch the candlelight play across her face the way it had back when the power was out. To see her without the stress of the wedding winding her tight and devouring her time. He wanted to have one—just one—leisurely dance with her. This mountain of chaos and obstacles had actually worked itself out into a wedding—wasn't that worth one dance?

"Mr. Bruce?"

"Huh?"

"You sure do go away in your head lots."

He looked at Lulu. "That's what Carly said she calls it," she went on. "Mom does something like that. Thinks real hard for a long time. She's been doing it loads since you showed up." She looked up at him with wide, "trying to look innocent" eyes. "What do you suppose that means?"

Bruce was grasping for an appropriate answer when Samantha's photographer clapped his hands. "Thank you, everyone," he called. "I'll see you over at the inn for the reception."

Carly came bouncing over to the pew. "Let's go. Miss Tina says I get to have our dance together first thing, even before dinner." She looked at Lulu. "We've been practicing and everything."

"Mom likes to dance, too," Lulu offered.

Carly grinned with the same "not quite innocent" look. "You're gonna dance with Lulu's mom, too, aren't you, Daddy?"

Bruce began to feel outnumbered and outmaneuvered. "We'll see." He forced himself to coat his tone with enough doubt to squelch this little campaign.

Lulu pouted. "My mom says it just like that, too."

"Where is your mother?" He tried to sound casual, as if he hadn't noticed the minute she left the sanctuary and felt the void left by her absence. He'd flown rescue squads with firefighters that required less strategy than the two girls currently flanking him.

"She had to take the church flowers over and turn them into things for the party tables 'cuz there wasn't enough for both," Lulu said, picking up her coat and handing Carly hers in alarmingly big-sister fashion. "I'll help you with that. See?" she said as she finished up Carly's jacket zipper. "Just like sisters." And with that, the two girls skipped up the church aisle holding hands.

He was grabbing his own coat when Tina and Darren came up behind him.

"Tina…" Bruce started.

She only smiled the blissful, dreamy smile of a new bride. "See you over at the inn."

Chapter Nineteen

She'd done it.

Well, they'd all done it, the whole valley, but when Samantha went on and on about the amazing way this wedding had come off and the glowing article she planned on writing, Kelly wanted to dance with joy.

Actually, she wanted to dance with Bruce. And laugh with him. And talk about God and love and loss and little girls with him. Oh, she and Bruce tried to put up a respectable amount of resistance to the obvious schemes of the girls, but it wasn't working. She was falling for him. Hard. And all the convincing she could muster about this being some kind of fantasy bubble certain to pop wasn't helping to stop her feelings one bit.

"How did they learn to do that at their age?" Bruce muttered with unconvincing annoyance as Lulu and Carly practically shoved them out together on the dance floor.

"I have no idea." Oh, why did he have to be such a good dancer? Different from Mark, but still wonderful. She'd always loved to dance, and hated being a "pity partner" of generous husbands at valley functions. "You can cut a rug, Mr. Lohan."

His face softened with memory. "Sandy loved to dance. Sorry, I'm probably way out of practice."

"No, you're not—no more than me anyway." After a moment, she said, "It's okay, you know. They're here."

"Who?"

"Mark. And Sandy. We were married to them. They're part of us, part of our daughters. They're here today, in a way, and that's okay." She dared a look up into his eyes. "How are you?"

His smile sent her heart to a host of unwise places. "Okay." After a moment, he took a shaky breath and said, "Fine. A surprising, scary kind of fine, actually." He stared into her eyes, and suddenly it was hard to feel the floor under her feet. "Kelly…"

If it wasn't the first time he said her name, it felt like it. Close and quiet, whispered like a secret. She both wanted him to say whatever was on the tip of his tongue, and dreaded any admission. It had to be the same thing she was thinking: *I'm scared. I'm unsure. I'm not ready. I've missed this so much.*

"Tuesday's coming," she managed to blurt out, citing the day he'd told her he and Carly would drive back home. The day reality would push its way back into their lives. The day that, right now, she couldn't bear the thought of coming.

His face fell. "Actually, Monday's coming. I haven't told Carly yet, but we have to leave a day early. The service called, and with the weather they're shorthanded and they need me back."

Kelly forced a casual, friendly tone to her voice. "And are you ready to go back? You said you'd taken the time off because things hadn't been going so well."

He gave her a lopsided, almost bittersweet smile that she found far too endearing. "I figured a few things out while I was here."

"I'm glad," she said, and it was mostly true. Glad he found some of the peace he sought, but unsettled by his readiness to return to the job she found so difficult to embrace. *Did You send this, God?* Kelly wondered to herself. *A reminder of what he does to knock some sense into me?* Mark's ever-changing schedule had been challenge enough. Bruce's job frequently dealt with unplanned emergencies, and could pull him away from her at any moment—or a crucial moment—leaving her alone. She didn't want to learn to depend on someone again only to have them called away by duty or disaster. Who could ever say, "I'm sorry about that forest fire or flood, but I could really use you here"?

"Hey," Bruce said, touching her cheek in a way that made her head spin, "I'm still here now. We have an amazing wedding reception to enjoy."

She knew what he was trying to say. To stop planning and analyzing and just enjoy the moment, relish her accomplishment. But being here, with Bruce, was so much more than that. No matter how lovely tonight might be, Monday would come. Monday always came. "I…"

"Carly told me last night she wanted to move here and be Lulu's little sister and grow up to run Marvin's ice-cream shop."

Kelly allowed herself a soft laugh. "She told me that, too. I like a girl who can plan."

Bruce looked over her shoulder, likely in the direction of where the girls were sitting. "What would you say if I told you I liked her plan?"

It wasn't fair what that question did to her.

All the wishing it unleashed. All the practicality it denied. All the very fragile hope it ignited. "How?" was all she could manage, and even that was more of a sigh than a word.

"I'm not sure," he said. His eyes told her he wanted to try, and she felt the last of her resistance crumbling away under the power of his gaze.

"I'm not sure, either," she replied, even as his arms tightened around her. How could she be sure of anything right now, except how delightful the moment felt and how much that delight scared her to death? If they were alone, she would have kissed him. And he would have kissed her back, and it would have been wonderful. But they were not alone—half the town was around them, and more important, the girls.

As if in defiance of that fact, the music slowed. Bruce pulled her close to him. "How about we just stop talking about it. Just put your head on my shoulder and enjoy the music."

Oh, the one thing sure to pull her under, the one thing she missed most of anything, was having a shoulder to lean against. The safe, blissful sensation of leaning her cheek against a strong shoulder. If any gesture meant "you're not alone" to her, it was that one. Kelly knew that if she allowed her head to rest against Bruce's shoulder, any hope of keeping sensible margins—of Bruce being just a customer or even just a friend—would be lost.

She'd faced down a storm, faced down a grouchy reporter, faced down a mountain of problems to see Darren and Tina married, but nothing felt as treacherous as the moment where Kelly tilted her head and felt Bruce's entire body change with the contact of her cheek against his collarbone.

Bruce's sigh was full of wonder and relief and fear. It sounded exactly like the tumble of sensations going through her heart. It was so much more than the embrace he'd given her in the hardware store. That one was careful and tentative. This one was full and strong and splendid. Her guard dropped even as his had, and she let herself lean into his strength. Kelly let herself be held up and swept across the floor by this man, this father, this soul seemingly so well matched to hers.

Did two dances go by or twelve? Kelly lost any professional sense of time and place, enthralled by the moment.

"Do you know what I'd give right now for Monday not to come?" he said softly.

She looked up at him, even though she knew it would spell the end of her resistance.

"Probably the same as what I'd give," she replied. "But Monday's coming anyway, isn't it?"

His eyes gleamed. "So let it. We just pulled off the most unlikely wedding in North Carolina. What's a Monday in the face of that?"

She pulled back just a bit to look at him. "You're serious."

"Look, I know Kinston's not exactly close. And I know what I do frightens you. But they're all just details in light of the big things, aren't they?"

"Those details *are* big things, Bruce." And they were.

"We've got bigger things. Four of 'em. And according to a certain florist I know, they're all we need." When she raised an eyebrow, he added, "In fact, we've got six by my count."

"Six?" Her heart felt like it tumbled over the falls with his words.

"A man, a woman, a valley, God and two amazing little girls. I'd pile that up against any set of logistics any day of the week." He gazed into her eyes with a certainty she'd not seen in him before this moment. "Would you?"

"You know," she said, reaching up to wrap her arms around his neck, "I believe I would."

His smile matched the glow she felt in her heart. "How should we tell the girls?"

"Like this," and with that, she titled her head up and kissed him. The room, the wedding and even the whole valley fell away from her awareness, leaving just the exquisite bliss of new love. A surprising, wondrous second chance she'd never seen coming.

Kelly thought it was her pulse pounding in her ears until she slowly realized it was clapping. And the gentle vibration of Bruce laughing as the elated yelps of two little girls filled her ears. She pulled away just enough to see the entire reception staring at them and applauding, led by Darren and Tina.

"Way to steal my thunder, Lohan," Darren said with a shameless grin.

"Sorry," Bruce said, sounding anything but.

"I'm not," Darren said, clasping Bruce on the back.

"We're not!" yelled Lulu and Carly in unison, jumping up and down. "Mom and Dad! Mom and Dad!"

"What is it about this valley?" Samantha Douglas said as she stood holding hands with Rob Folston.

"I don't know," Bruce said, holding Kelly's hand tight. "But I sure am going to stick around long enough to find out."

Epilogue

"So," Yvonne said, leaning over the bakery counter, "now that I know why there's a bunch of hearts hanging in your shop window, I want to hear every single detail."

"Well," said Kelly, feeling a bit breathless, "we were at the airport in Charlotte—"

"Wait a minute," Yvonne cut in, straightening up. "We've got the most beautiful waterfall in the state right out back and he takes you to the *airport*?"

Kelly tried to scowl, but her sheer joy just wouldn't let her pull it off. She planted her hands playfully on her hips instead. "Are you going to let me tell the story or what?"

In reply, Yvonne leaned both elbows on the bakery counter and planted her chin in her hands, a dramatic "I'm all ears" pose if there ever was one.

"So we went up in one of the helicopters he flies for his new job. He said we were going to Raleigh to buy baby gifts for Jean's shower next week."

"Baby Julia will be here before we know it. Jean's as big as a house. I've been kidding her they need to confirm it's not twins. But don't get off the subject. So you're up in a helicopter…" She made a skeptical face. "Noise, altitude, headphones…"

"They're a private fleet," Kelly replied, "so these helicopters are very nice. But I knew something was up when we headed west instead of east. Bruce took me up over the mountains. And you know what a pretty summer day it was yesterday."

"Gorgeous," Yvonne agreed, "but you're in a helicopter."

Granted, most people wouldn't consider the setting romantic, but to her it was perfect. "He said he wanted to be absolutely sure I'd made my peace with the sky." That was the wonder of Bruce. He understood her—her history, her weaknesses, all of her—completely. "And while I thought I had, at that moment I *knew* I had. And I told him so, but of course I was crying when I did."

"That is rather sweet. I'll give him that," Yvonne said.

"And he told me that while he was glad to have given me back the sky, I'd given him the whole world back. That he was sure he'd never find joy again but he was so happy now. And that he knew lots of men got down on one knee, but he wanted to ask me to marry him up among the clouds." She stared at the stunning sky blue sapphire solitaire that now graced her left hand, surrounded by a "cloud" of white diamonds. Blue sky and clouds, at her fingertips for the rest of her life. It was the most romantic thing she could ever imagine.

"And you said…" Yvonne clued, wide-eyed and smiling.

"Of course I said yes," Kelly gushed. "And I kissed him as much as two headphones and air traffic safely protocols would allow."

"Which I expect wasn't much."

Kelly blushed. "We made up for it once we landed."

"Of course. And the girls?"

"They were waiting up when we got home. Bruce had written them both letters saying what he was doing. It was adorable, really." She yawned. "We all stayed up far too late being ridiculously happy."

"Good for you," Yvonne said, coming around the counter to admire the beautiful ring. "Matrimony Valley pairs off another one of its fine women. And I get to make another cake."

"You do," Kelly agreed, hugging her friend. "But be warned, I plan to throw my bouquet straight at you."

Yvonne pulled away just a bit. "Oh, yeah? How's your aim?"

Kelly discovered she could smile even wider. "Excellent."

* * * * *

If you enjoyed this story, go back to check out the first heartwarming romance in the Matrimony Valley series:

His Surprise Son

Find these and other great reads at www.LoveInspired.com

Dear Reader,

Comebacks are hard. Restoring hope is an uphill battle for so many of us, especially when life knocks us down. Ah, but God moves most mightily in the uphill battles, and He is a splendid restorer. Often, His restorations bring back to us even more than we had before. That certainly is true for Bruce and Kelly—and adorable Carly and Lulu—and my prayer is that it is true for you, as well.

If this is your first visit to Matrimony Valley, go back and discover *His Surprise Son*, where Mayor Jean has her own family restored beyond her wildest expectations. And look forward to the next book in the Matrimony Valley series, where baker Yvonne Niles finds her own recipe for happiness.

I love to hear from readers, so please connect with me on Facebook or Twitter, email me at *allie@alliepleiter.com* or use good old-fashioned post at P.O. Box 7026, Villa Park, IL 60181.

Blessings,
Allie

Get 4 FREE REWARDS!

We'll send you 2 FREE Books plus 2 FREE Mystery Gifts.

Love Inspired® Suspense books feature Christian characters facing challenges to their faith... and lives.

FREE Value Over **$20**

YES! Please send me 2 FREE Love Inspired® Suspense novels and my 2 FREE mystery gifts (gifts are worth about $10 retail). After receiving them, if I don't wish to receive any more books, I can return the shipping statement marked "cancel." If I don't cancel, I will receive 4 brand-new novels every month and be billed just $5.24 each for the regular-print edition or $5.74 each for the larger-print edition in the U.S., or $5.74 each for the regular-print edition or $6.24 each for the larger-print edition in Canada. That's a savings of at least 13% off the cover price. It's quite a bargain! Shipping and handling is just 50¢ per book in the U.S. and 75¢ per book in Canada*. I understand that accepting the 2 free books and gifts places me under no obligation to buy anything. I can always return a shipment and cancel at any time. The free books and gifts are mine to keep no matter what I decide.

Choose one: ☐ **Love Inspired® Suspense**
Regular-Print
(153/353 IDN GMY5)

☐ **Love Inspired® Suspense**
Larger-Print
(107/307 IDN GMY5)

Name (please print)

Address   Apt. #

City   State/Province   Zip/Postal Code

Mail to the **Reader Service:**
IN U.S.A.: P.O. Box 1341, Buffalo, NY 14240-8531
IN CANADA: P.O. Box 603, Fort Erie, Ontario L2A 5X3

Want to try two free books from another series? Call 1-800-873-8635 or visit www.ReaderService.com.

*Terms and prices subject to change without notice. Prices do not include applicable taxes. Sales tax applicable in N.Y. Canadian residents will be charged applicable taxes. Offer not valid in Quebec. This offer is limited to one order per household. Books received may not be as shown. Not valid for current subscribers to Love Inspired Suspense books. All orders subject to approval. Credit or debit balances in a customer's account(s) may be offset by any other outstanding balance owed by or to the customer. Please allow 4 to 6 weeks for delivery. Offer available while quantities last.

Your Privacy—The Reader Service is committed to protecting your privacy. Our Privacy Policy is available online at www.ReaderService.com or upon request from the Reader Service. We make a portion of our mailing list available to reputable third parties that offer products we believe may interest you. If you prefer that we not exchange your name with third parties, or if you wish to clarify or modify your communication preferences, please visit us at www.ReaderService.com/consumerschoice or write to us at Reader Service Preference Service, P.O. Box 9062, Buffalo, NY 14240-9062. Include your complete name and address.

LIS18

Get 4 FREE REWARDS!

We'll send you 2 FREE Books plus 2 FREE Mystery Gifts.

Harlequin® Heartwarming™ Larger-Print books feature traditional values of home, family, community and most of all—love.

FREE
Value Over
$20

HOME *on the* RANCH

READERSERVICE.COM

Manage your account online!
- Review your order history
- Manage your payments
- Update your address

> ### *We've designed the Reader Service website just for you.*

Enjoy all the features!
- Discover new series available to you, and read excerpts from any series.
- Respond to mailings and special monthly offers.
- Browse the Bonus Bucks catalog and online-only exculsives.
- Share your feedback.

Visit us at:

ReaderService.com